Destiel

by

Jordyn Burlot

For My Angel

Acknowledgement

Thank you to the amazing person in my life
who made me believe I could write.
You're a superstar and I love you with all my heart.
I hope, one day, you will know how
special you are…

Destiel

Some people are just worth

giving up everything for...

Prologue

I reach his hotel room in the early hours. The low orange light from the table lamp flickers upon my arrival, causing a warm glow to dance across his pale complexion. He is on top of the bedding and I notice his ripped shirt lying on the floor next to him. I wonder what has happened to cause the tear, and then I am distracted by his creamy, satin skin. He is sleeping but not soundly. I know the lowest of sinister whispers will rouse him in an instant, and his hand, which is nestled beneath his pillow, will pull his gun. My heart races as I watch the rhythm of his chest while he breathes deeply. He's alone, he's always alone these days. I long to lay beside him and whisper how I feel but I cannot. I hold my thoughts together. I have to. I know I can never earn back my Wayfarer's Wings if I give in to this temptation. I will remain without my powers, my grace of flight, abandoned and imprisoned within my own imperfection...

I prioritise my feelings and somehow detach myself from my desire. I look uneasily around the room and wonder how he is able to separate the sounds of true danger from the roar of traffic outside. The crude shouts from undesirable drunks who pass by his window would be enough to prompt the average person to be a little concerned, but not him. He's different, he doesn't fear the echoes of the night as others do. He has come to know that true human vulnerability arises from what is unnatural. There is nothing he fears more than solitude, yet he lives and works alone. This place is base and unclean. He doesn't belong here, and it is almost intolerable for me to see his sensitive nature corroded by his sense of duty. A human being should never be exposed to half of what he has seen. I know that this lifestyle will eventually extinguish all purity.

I see his packed bag, waiting by the door for a quick exit. This is no existence and no way for him to live. The bitter taste of reality helps me to focus, and I feel my restless spirit soothe as a gush of endurance floods through my body. My blood runs cold as my passion is pushed aside, but I know it has to be this way. I take a few deep breaths before calling to him…

"Sean, why aren't you doing something?" I say loudly, knowing my voice will rouse him from sleep.

"Destiel?" he replies, squinting, as his eyes scan the room, his gaze eventually settling on my face. "Where the Hell have you been?" he snaps as he brushes his hand across his brow. I am lost for words, I knew this question would come but I have no way to pacify his anger towards me. I know I have let him down badly. He groans and I watch as he stands up, crosses the room to his bag and pulls out a black tee shirt. "Well?" he says before throwing it on over his head and heading back to his bed. He picks up his watch, "Do you have any idea what time it is?" he sighs as he flings it carelessly aside and flops back down.

"You haven't answered my question, Sean. Why aren't you doing anything? People are dying," I ask with feigned force. He lays down with his hands upstretched behind his head. At first, it seems he is exasperated. I wait for his temper to erupt but then, to my surprise, I notice his eyes close. He appears to have fallen straight back to sleep.

"Sean," I shout, furiously, at his blatant lack of concern.

"What do you want, Destiel," he growls as he opens his eyes again. He seems different.

"You have to take care of it, Sean. I see your shirt is torn, have you encountered it?" I ask.

"Huh? I don't know what you're talking about," he grumbles before sitting up and stretching. I notice his shirt ride up slightly as he does so. I instantly avert my eyes and clear my mind of all impure thoughts before turning, purposefully, back to face him. "What?" he snaps, upon noticing my arms fold as I raise my eyebrows and give him *that* look. "I don't need this, Destiel," he huffs. "Who do you think you are? Coming round here in the middle of the freakin' night and telling me..."

"Sean, that thing is out there, it's not going to stop," I interrupt quickly, not wanting to explain where I have been and why I have not answered him in so long. I heard his distressed pleas. I knew he was calling... calling out to me. I ached to give into his desperate requests but I knew my feelings were forbidden. My emotions were becoming so much harder to suppress and I knew I was on the verge of giving in to my yearning to be with him. This is the true reason I could not come to him. If only he felt the same way... maybe... just maybe I could walk away from it all... for him...

"Thing? What thing?" he says, raising his voice above my thoughts. "I've had enough of this crap. I've been calling you, I needed you here, where were you?" He stares me right in the eye and I find it impossible to lie to him.

"I know, Sean. It's not important right now," I reply hastily as I turn my back on him. How can I tell him I begged not to come here tonight, that I need to stay away, that I'm worn out resisting the temptation to tell him how I feel. I breathe deeply as I compose myself.

"This thing is not going to stop until it's ripped out the throat of every woman on Earth," I say with an air of authority barely strong enough to be convincing.

Sean sighs hard. He knows he's not going to get a straight answer from me, and I sense him lie back down on the bed, "You wanna enlighten me?" he groans in disappointment.

"I have come about the Sior-Mabuz, Sean," I reply as I wonder how he cannot know about this thing.

"Sior – what?"

"Sior-Mabuz," I repeat.

"I don't know what you're talking about, Destiel. Who sent it?"

"It didn't come through the time portal. Well, not recently anyway. This is one of the original constructs. An early one. It has been around for many centuries. It is a mutation. It somehow managed to become fused with a human."

"How come I don't know about it then?"

"It has been imprisoned for many years. I wasn't aware it had escaped," I tell him as a certain amount of shame causes me to regret my part in it all. How can I say I am partially to blame for its escape? That I should have been more vigilant in my checks upon this creature's imprisonment?

"Escaped? From where?"

"During the Dark Ages it was captured in what we now know as England. It was named Sior, on account of its daytime hunting regime. Once detained, it was transported to Scotland, where it became known as Sior-Mabuz – 'the sun feeder of death castle'. It was the only one of its kind ever, and it can never be destroyed…"

"Oh great," Sean snorts.

"Just listen," I snap. "I can't do your job for you, Sean. You're the agent, you do it. The best we can hope for is that it be contained, confined to darkness for all eternity. It has been locked up in a dungeon in the Scottish Highlands, up until now that is. I have located its whereabouts to this town. I guessed its presence was the reason you were here, you need to isolate it and…" I hear the sound of snoring and turn to find Sean asleep.

I pace the room. I'm confused, he is obviously exhausted but I have no idea why. I move right up close to the bed and kneel in front of him. I feel his breath on my face and I close my eyes and allow myself to imagine for a moment. My thoughts take me far away to my special dream, where we are together, in love and happy. My body tingles in the illusion and my troubled heart finds peace, but I know this cannot be, and I drag myself reluctantly from my pipedream. I open my eyes and stare longingly into his beautiful face. I wish so much that he were mine. I wish I had the courage to tell him how I feel but I'm a coward. I know I must leave now but for some reason I cannot move. The love inside is too strong. How can I overcome my desire for this man. It's too hard. It's impossible, nobody could live with the torture I feel inside of me. Why must I go through this time and time again? Destined to be near him but fated never to be one with him.

My whole body fills with sorrow as I move my lips close to him. I am millimetres from his mouth and I yearn for him to awake and pull me to him and tell me everything will be okay because he loves me too. I loiter there and wait for him to make my fantasy reality, to lift me to the stars with his soft embrace, but it doesn't happen. I know I must go, and I order my mind to discipline itself. I whisper softly into his ear, "Goodnight, Sean." I move away from him and approach the door. I glance back only once, and then I am gone.

Chapter 1

"What are you doing here, Sean?" I ask as I walk into the bar and find him slouched over a table, his half-eaten meal pushed aside. He drops the bottle he is loosely holding and I hear a distinct crack as it hits the floor. He seems very jumpy tonight. I wonder what's wrong, but then I remember, there is always *something* wrong.

"What?" he replies, yawning before throwing me an annoyed glance. I sit down next to him.

"It's still on the loose, Sean. It has been over a week now, why hasn't it been contained?" I ask urgently. He completely ignores me, instead taking it upon himself to yell out for more beer. No one is listening and so, with a shrug, he gives up. I watch as he places his head in his hand and closes his eyes. I wait for him to reply to my question. When he doesn't, I go to the bar and get him another drink. I return to his table, sit down and nudge him. He shakes me away with a push.

"Sean!" I say sternly as I shove his drink in front of him.

"What?" he snaps, throwing me another angry glare.

"Sean, why are you here?"

"I'm looking for someone." He holds up his hand. "Don't even ask," he replies moodily as he picks up his beer, takes a large gulp and wipes his mouth on his sleeve.

"Why haven't you found it, Sean? It should have been captured."

"Because Share MyBooze, or whatever, must have left, it's not here," he scoffs as he goes back to chugging on his beer. I can't stand it when he gets this way. I feel like dragging him out of here and pounding some sense into him.

"It killed three people yesterday, Sean," I say, shoving the newspaper under his nose.

"What?" he replies, seeming to have sobered up within the space of a few seconds. "Hold on a minute, it says here: *It fed on her like some kind of vampire.* Vampire, really?" He raises his eyebrows and thrusts the paper away from himself. "This is the first I've seen of this, and I can't find out anything from *anyone* around here," he whispers as he surreptitiously scans around. "The people in this town are freakin' *freaks*. You try talking to them."

"No, Sean. You talk to them, and it's called the Sior-Mabuz. It feeds on women - not for food, but for thrills and form maintenance. It is *not* a vampire. People are becoming hysterical, Sean. They are jumping to all sorts of fantastical conclusions. This needs to end. Now."

"Form maintenance? What does that even mean?"

"It needs to feed in order to obtain power. This is how it sustains its appearance. It's a vicious cycle, and one that Sior-Mabuz is completely unaware of. It feeds on impulse. It feeds to regenerate. It needs energy, which it uses to replenish the skin cells of the host subject it occupies. It does this in order to remain...

14

attractive to females, so that it may begin the cycle again. It doesn't feed in order to survive, it feeds to maintain the illusion of flesh and blood."

"So it doesn't have to bother killing then, it would just exist anyway?"

"Yes. It is part machine after all. It is unaware… or perhaps it just enjoys the pursuit. Sean, you must…"

"Who is it after?"

"It's not after anyone, Sean. It has long since forgotten its mission."

"What mission?"

"I am unsure exactly, but I assume it was originally sent back to kill someone before they were born, thus preventing some future event."

"Did it succeed?"

"I do not know but it was injured and so there must have been a fight. What I can tell you, is that it felt the need to mutate. This is when it merged with the human in order to save itself. When it did so, it became completely oblivious to its own purpose and nature. It needs to be dealt with, and quickly."

"I'm worn-out, Dest. Can't you do it? Zone in on it and beam it back or whatever?"

"I no longer have those powers, Sean, you know that. I cannot travel through time and space anymore. I have, let's say, been relieved of duties."

"And why is that exactly? Why are you locked out of your own time machine?"

"I told you, Sean, my emotions rendered me incapable of doing my job. I couldn't protect the world like that. A Wayfarer cannot keep his mind on what he needs to do if his thoughts are elsewhere. Besides, it would be unethical of me to put my own desires before the natural course of history. I am in a position of trust. I need to prove myself worthy again and that takes time."

"You had time, you had a freakin' time machine… Anyway, who actually was it you were…"

"It doesn't work like that," I say, swiftly halting the conversation. "Sean, you must isolate…"

"Right," he snaps, standing up and swaying slightly, "How do I destroy it?"

"You don't. You can't. It's immortal, truly immortal." He sits down again and turns to me, his green eyes darting in panic as his bottom lip quivers slightly. He feels guilty. If there's one thing he can't stand, it's letting people down. I feel his guilt. He leans forward, rests his elbow on the table and looks straight at me. I'm mesmerised as I move towards him, I feel intoxicated. I close my eyes and await his kiss and…

"Come on, Dest, let's get the bastard," he slurs as he slaps the top of my arm, rushes off, returns for what's left of his burger, smiles with a mouthful of food and zooms off again.

I start after him, "Sean, you can't do this tonight, wait until tomorrow," I call to him as I watch him fling his food to the floor. I know there is something bothering him. I can sense these things, but there's a stony wall keeping me from seeing what's inside.

I give up on talking him out of it. There's no way he's going to let it go. Looks like I'm stuck here with him on this one for the night. I can't leave him alone now for fear of him coming to harm. I let out a deep sigh and follow him. Needless to say, we achieve nothing.

A few hours later, after wandering aimlessly, I attempt to reason with him again.

"Let's go, Sean, we're getting nowhere," I say as I turn to face him, and then dive for cover as I witness his face contort into the most revolting creature imaginable. The sun has come up and I realize Sean *is* the Sior-Mabuz. I get myself together, somehow manage to pull my weapon and stun him. He staggers and, for a time, seems disorientated. However, it doesn't take long before the swaying stops, and he resists the effects of the blast long enough to be aware of my presence and my attack. The Sior-Mabuz howls and I know it is going to target my neck. I have to be quick, one swipe and it's over. I launch myself in its direction as I attempt to unbalance the thing. It is unprepared for such an ambush and, in the struggle, I am successful in overcoming its brute strength. I shock him again and he falls to the ground. Then, the Sior-Mabuz, in its effort to preserve itself, goes into spontaneous hibernation and its own image is lost. Once again, I see Sean's face. I waste no time. I haul the thing back to Sean's accommodation before it regains consciousness and transforms into its true configuration once again.

I wait patiently for night to come, knowing that the monster within Sean will fall silent and the guy I love will come back to me. I can barely look at his twisted contortion of a body. The effects of the shock did not take long to wear off and now he lies tied to the floor joists, screaming insults at me. His repulsive mouth runs with some sort of saliva, something I can only describe as black bile broth. He is repugnant to me. How it got inside Sean, I do not know. I am thankful for the noisy motel as his language and hissing is foul enough to wake the dead. The busy road and service station outside serves as a distraction to those walking by, allowing the noise of the creature to go unnoticed. I cannot bear this. I cannot stand to see Sean this way. I know I must save him and bring him back from wherever he is, but he is now so hard to reach. I know the Sior-Mabuz can never be exterminated, and I know that whomever it inhabits will remain the Sior-Mabuz for all eternity. Not even death can release its grip and, unless the Sior-Mabuz finds another host, *it* and its subject are enmeshed, and the human soul of its host is trapped forever...

But... surely... there must be a way. Any attempt at getting the creature to take another vessel in the past did not go well. I can't risk it again, I'm just not ready to lose him. There must be some other way, surely. If there is, I shall find it. I know, for now, that the Sior-Mabuz must be returned to its dwelling place, deep within the dungeon of Hielan De'il Stravaig Castle, and there it must remain. I fear Sean will never be free again, and he will never again be the Sean - the breath-taking Sean - I love and desire with all my heart.

"Sean, wake up," I say after sundown. He is now *my* Sean once again. His beautiful face has returned, and the Sior-Mabuz is asleep, deep within. I now know why Sean is reluctant to eat. Food is poison to this entity. I also know the reason that Sean is so very tired. The beast consumes vitality and the subject, for the most part, is comatose. Perhaps it is a blessing this is so.

"Sean," I whisper as I get close to him. He opens his eyes. He appears drained and I help him to sit up.

"What the…" he gasps as he notices the chains locked around his body. I stare anxiously for a moment as he tugs against them in a vain attempt to free himself.

"Please, Sean, please stop," I shush him gently as I hold him tight until his frustration subsides. "You are chained because the Sior-Mabuz is within you. This is for your own safety, and that of others. I cannot allow it to continue killing, Sean. Surely, you know this. You must feel it inside you?"

He looks into my eyes and I know he has understood this bleak truth. His own eyes fill with tears and, before I know it, his frame becomes crumpled as he reaches for me and pulls me close to him. The terrible erratic rhythm of his heart resounds through my entire body and, at once, my heart follows his and beats in time to his song of anguish. I allow the embrace to take place as I attempt to distance myself and pull back from my longing to become one with him. It is an act of discipline like no other.

Eventually, he moves away from me. Tear tracks stain his bloodied and bruised face and I see a vulnerability I have never witnessed in him before. It would be easy for me to take advantage of such an occasion, an occasion that will most likely never come my way again, but I refrain. I will remain good. I have to. I know this can never happen or I will be forced to remain in this time zone forever, never again being allowed to return to my own time.

"What exactly is this thing? It hurts so bad," he whispers.

"Sean, you have to stay focussed. Your pain will subside." He looks at me and takes a deep breath as he holds his side. I am aware that it was me who caused him to be in pain. The hit penetrated the Sior-Mabuz and affected Sean's body also. He seems to relax and then raises his hands as if he is in complete acceptance of the situation. "Are you okay?" I ask him.

"Look, I get it's something from the future. Is *this* what humans turn into?"

"No, Sean, it is not a future human. I told you before, this a machine-human hybrid. It came back many years ago. Somehow, it was damaged and that's when it merged with a human. It gained superior strength from its newly formed union – becoming almost super-powered. We are not sure how it fused with the man but we assume it was at cellular level. Fortunately, its new semi-organic structure meant it could not get back to its own time. Probably just as well. If it had managed to travel back to its own century then its knowledge would have certainly been used

20

against us, and humanity would exist only as host bodies for these things. I'm sorry it found you, Sean."

"Are you telling me I have some pre-historic guy in me as well?"

"Yes, he and it are now the same entity and this is why it shares similar raw human desires. It will never part with this man. He *is* the original subject, they are now fused. Human and machine together as one, forget the movies, Sean. This is the real face of transhumanism - an honest portrayal, you might say."

"Huh?" he says appearing confused. He wipes his hand across his face, "well, that's just great." He looks exhausted. "Why me, Dest? I mean, what… did it seek me out personally?" he sighs, and I tell him what I know.

"The Sior-Mabuz requires a certain… magnetism… and… well… you fulfil that requirement, shall we say."

"So, I'm good looking, is that what you're saying… hang on a minute… didn't I turn into some grotesque beast?" He laughs, and the vulnerability is gone.

"Yes. It is able to use your appearance at will. You serve many purposes. Your image allows it to move around without drawing attention to itself. It serves also as a trap to lure women away from the crowds. Not only this, but your body is an adequate disguise when it sleeps. It prefers to use your image, but it will use its own form when it is alone or feels threatened."

"And there was me thinking it was *just* a monster!" He rests his chin on his hand. "So it's cunning and manipulative then… pretty smart yeah?"

"Yes, it can be. Just like a person can be. There are similarities. This twisted predator is able to access the knowledge inside your head. It's a mutated machine remember, and your service record during the temporal war speaks for itself. You have garnered a reputation over the years. You are simply the ideal candidate."

"Well, I wish I hadn't bothered. What good has it done anyway? These mechanical bastards are set on destroying this planet no matter what you or I do. People think this war is over, but I know it's just the beginning. I'll tell you something else too - now you're out of commission, we're doomed anyway. They will never let it rest. Just let this thing kill me. At least then it'll be dead."

"No, it won't. It will continue to animate and regenerate your replenished corpse whilst your soul lies trapped, witnessing each and every mindless slaughter…"

"Oh, that's just great. I'm going to be an apocalyptic zombie." He turns sharply towards me, "Why don't you ever have any *good* news? I'll tell you what, why don't you just shut up for a while, huh?"

"Hey, it's not my fault it chose you."

"Well whose fault is it then, mine?"

"I'm trying to help. You might show some gratitude"

"Well excuse me if I don't jump for joy."

"Sean, this is getting us nowhere. We need to get it back to Scotland and quickly."

"So there's something there that can help us then? Well, let's go, the sooner the better. How do I actually get this thing out of me?" he asks impatiently with a spark of optimism.

"You don't. You will remain imprisoned there in the dungeon forever."

"You're kidding me, right?"

"No."

"What was that I was saying about good news? Next you'll be telling me I'll be on a diet of deep fried haggis forever."

"Don't tempt me, Sean."

"Destiel, let me out of this contraption right now," he says tugging on the chains. "I'm going to find a way to get rid of this bastard... sorry... *these* bastards." He throws me an acid look before rattling the chains harder than before. I understand his frustration but I will not let him out. "I'm screwed if I'm going to be one of the walking dead," he insists. I shake my head in refusal. "I'll do this with or without your help," he says as he pushes me to one side and, once again, attempts to escape the manacles.

"No, Sean. You *will* return to Hielan De'il Stravaig Castle, and there you *will* stay."

"Who made you boss? Some friend you are," he says as he turns and, within an instant, falls asleep. He's completely drained. Nobody could withstand such a trauma. He's lucky to be alive.

I decide to let him nap for a while, perhaps later he will see reason and understand. I gently slide a pillow beneath his head and cover him with a blanket before leaving the room. I need to find the best way to get him to Scotland whilst the sun is down. I cannot risk him becoming the Sior-Mabuz on our journey. I silently leave the room. I need to clear my head in the hopes of coming up with a plan to get us out of here.

When I return, I find that Sean has vanished. I pick up the manacle and see that it has been sawn through. I glance around and see the tools, which have been pulled from beneath the bed. I have no idea how he reached them but I know he must be stopped. I dash from the room. I must find him before daybreak.

I know he cannot use his car as I have transported it many miles away. He will not find it. I check every transit point within the area, but do not find him. Perhaps he is hiding from me, watching me from a secret location and waiting it out until I leave, but I do not sense him near. Fortunately, I am blessed with second sight. This is one of the reasons I was chosen for the mission of righting the wrongs of the past. Our aim is to prevent the war, which is constantly being postponed, only to be resume again once peace is found. Will these battles ever end, will we ever be free? My hopes for that have faded over the years. I believe I will always be destined to travel through time, mission after mission, never settling for long. That's if I ever prove myself worthy again and am allowed back to my own time. I miss home.

I sit down on a bench for a moment, I need to think. Where would he go? Sean isn't stupid, and he isn't cruel. This is why I know he will not attempt to leave on foot. He will not risk being a danger to anyone, let alone allow himself to be a murder catalyst. He will secure himself before sun up. That much I know, but I am also aware that he will not return the Sior-Mabuz to the dungeon without first finding a solution - a solution I know is beyond his reach. In desperation, I go from bar to bar, restaurant to restaurant, although I know he is not hungry for human food. I find almost every eatery closed and the bars in darkness. I know he's looking for answers and it kills me inside to imagine his desperation. I should have known he would escape, why didn't I stay with him? Never again will I leave his side. My poor, lost, Sean.

I am at a loss to know what to do and so I take a walk beyond the town to clear my mind. I need peace to tune into the vibrations around me. I don't have much time, the sun will rise very soon. I need to detach myself from all thoughts of his anguish to see clearly. I walk the lanes and eventually stumble upon an old abandoned town. It must be the old village, long since abandoned by the passage of time. I feel him near. I keep emotionally distant as I become physically closer to him, and then I see it, a deserted mausoleum. I walk down the steps, the smell is distracting but I continue. The whole place is soundless to the untrained ear, but I am able to detect the breath of a hiding soul. The pulsation is unmistakable and I would know it anywhere.

"Come out, Sean. I know you're here," I say, my voice quaking. He makes no sound. "Sean," I repeat. "You cannot hide from me."

He emerges from the shadows, and his slumped frame slowly approaches me. His pain is unbearable to me.

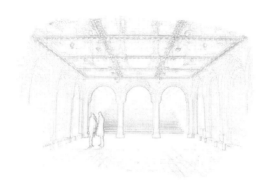

"I don't know what to do, Dest," he says softly.

"Let me help you, Sean. I *will* find a way, but we must leave for Scotland soon." He nods in agreement. "Why are you here, Sean," I ask, looking around and gesturing to the cold, dank building.

"The sun can't reach me here," he replies with a shrug. "It's all I could find to hide out in."

"The Sior-Mabuz has an internal clock, Sean. You *will* change."

"Dest, what can I do?" he says, grabbing my shoulder as he stares at the ground, desperately trying to hide the tears welling in his eyes. I feel overwhelmed

26

by my sorrow over his plight. I want to look after him and keep him safe. The longer this goes on the less chance I have of him remaining himself. If it cannot feed, it cannot rejuvenate Sean's skin cells.

"We need to barricade ourselves inside," I say as I hold his arm and pull him towards me.

"Thank you, Dest... for helping me, I mean," he says as he raises his head and conjures a weak smile. There's something different in his eyes and, for a brief second, we connect in a mellow, sensual way. He feels something for me, I see it in his glistening stare. I grab him tightly and hold him close. I feel his soft, brown hair caress my face and I am overcome with desire. I lean into him and kiss the top of his head, drinking in the moment. He holds me closer, breathing heavily, as I feel his hand slide down my back, and then it is over. I feel a bitter sense of loss as he pulls away and urges me to act quickly if we are to ensure he does not escape. We set to work.

Chapter 2

We decide to remain where we are for the time being. The location is ideal and, having set an appropriate barrier to the outside world, we are able to contain the Sior-Mabuz undetected. I have no option but let go of my vow to stay by his side. I need to leave Sean alone during the day as I attempt to find a way for us to get to Scotland. Something has to be done. I believe he will now cooperate fully. It is not going to be easy as we cannot allow Sean to come into contact with people, especially women, during the hours of daylight.

The following evening, when he awakes as himself, we make a fire to keep warm while we talk over the plans for our expedition.

"Sean, the only way I see for you to travel unnoticed is by oil tanker. It will take around a week for you to arrive. We must somehow find a way to restrain you aboard."

"Huh?"

"Yes, I will fly alone and prepare a location for your arrival. We can hide out there before making the journey to Hielan De'il Stravaig."

"Okay, let me get this straight, I haul up on a manky hull, while you snuggle up in a cosy hotel room?"

"Yes," I reply as Sean rolls his eyes. I sense he's not happy with this arrangement.

"I have a better idea, why don't you go and get the times of the flights to Scotland and see if there's one that leaves and arrives overnight?" He raises his eyebrows as he waits for my response.

"This is a good idea, Sean, but what if there is a delay at the airport?"

"Well, we're just going to have to take that chance because I'm not spending a stinking, oily week caught somewhere between here and Europe."

"You'd be asleep most of the time and…"

"Shut up, Destiel. Just get the times of the flights." He throws his jacket over my head, and I pull it away to see him smiling and I smile back. The smouldering shadows from the flames now flicker across his face and he is more striking than ever before. I cannot pull my eyes from him.

I agree to his request and later, once morning arrives, I check the Sior-Mabuz is secure. I then make my exit, leaving the beast frothing at the mouth as it tries to escape from its restraints. I cannot be away long, this I know. I head straight to the town, to the first agent I can find, to book plane tickets. I am lucky, there is a flight from New York to Glasgow leaving the following night. This will give us chance to travel to

New York and hide out before take-off. I consider delay but I know time is not on our side.

I collect Sean's car and head straight back to him and then wait out the hours for nightfall to arrive so I can tell him the news. The noise from the creature is almost deafening and the vibration makes me nauseous. I step outside, glad to be away from the thing. I hover there until all is quiet and then head back inside to find Sean awake. I make him as comfortable as I can before telling him the news.

"Sean, it's an eight hour flight. Departing at 7.30pm and landing in Glasgow at 7.30am, local time. We need to be at the airport at 5.30pm. If we are close enough, you will have time to change back into yourself, just before we need to leave for the flight."

Sean nods. "I know a pretty secure place we can stay at near the airport, about twenty minutes away. Can we do it? What time do I become me again?"

"Around 5 o'clock, so we have half an hour to get to the airport. This should not be a problem, Sean."

"Right, well, that's okay this end but it'll be morning there. What if I hulk out on the plane?"

"No, Sean, Scotland is still dark in the morning at this time of year. That thing runs according to the hours of darkness and light. It senses the changes wherever it is. We will have around an hour to get you ensconced into an abandoned building there."

"What if there *are* none?"

"I know the area. The east side, where we will be, is… let's say… a little unsavoury. I've done this journey before."

"So this is a regular occurrence to you?" Sean gasps with an amused look about him.

"No, I've been there before when I was tracking a machine traveller. Believe *me*, Sean, in this place, if you were to hulk out as you put it, the locals might not even notice the difference." I tease, hoping to get my intended response.

"You crack me up, Dest," he laughs and I feel happy to have cheered him up.

We set off immediately, the journey should take no more than three hours. I am sceptical but Sean believes we have time. I hope so. I stare out of the window most of the way. I'm so tired, I've barely slept for days. There was once a time when sleep was almost unnecessary for me and I can still go longer than the average person without it, but this is killing me. I look at Sean and he seems to be himself, but I know that thing is in there, waiting to explode into life the following morning. I close my eyes briefly, and immerse myself in a sleepy moment of nostalgia. As unpleasant as the surroundings might have been, our embrace in the mausoleum was the most romantic moment of my life and I allow myself to replay it in my mind's eye. I begin to drift off to sleep, comforted by the memory, when I am jolted awake by the lights of an oncoming car.

"Sean, I need to sleep, I'm sorry," I say as I once again close my eyes. The next thing I know, we are there.

"Wakey, wakey, sleeping beauty," I hear Sean say as he shakes me awake. I turn, sticky eyed, and notice he looks different. I need to get him inside before he changes. "Welcome to The Hilton," he laughs with an unnerving cackle that echoes through the night and continues eerily on whilst I run to the trunk of the car and get the chains out. I then head back around the side of the car to find Sean staggering up the path of the disused factory. I pursue him and manage to grab him before he falls. His face is becoming twisted. I look up to see the sun has begun to come up and I wish we could have left it a few more days before making the journey. "Help me, Dest, I'm not going to make it," he gasps. I use all my strength to lift him and, in my distress, I manage to carry him inside.

I glance around to find something solid I can chain him to. I spot a metal hook in the wall and make towards it as I hear a gruff, vulgar voice. It orders me to leave the premises. I stop in my tracks and turn around to see, what I assume to be, a group of addicts desperately trying to defend their territorial turf. They see me holding Sean but I ignore the sneers as I continue to head for the hook, and then I find myself surrounded these people. I don't know what to do and chaos descends. My panic is unwarranted as the Sior-Mabuz awakes and my problem is resolved. One of them is seized, and his throat unceremoniously removed in the most degrading of fashions. The others flee as quickly as possible and, in the raucous, I am able to sling the chain around Sior-Mabuz and lock it into the peg. It then turns to me and I have no escape. I cover my eyes as I wait for it to unleash its vengeance on me but nothing comes. I uncover my eyes again to find it staring at me with our faces almost touching, but still it does nothing. I stand still, my whole body shaking with terror and then, for a split second, I notice a shadow cross its eyes and I know it will not hurt me.

33

I move aside as it turns its attention to the doorway, to where the men made their escape. I then sink wearily to the floor as I watch it go into a frenzy as it attempts to escape and chase the men.

It's still roaring and tugging hours later and I want so much for that sound to stop. If I could kill it, I would, just to shut the thing up. I hide the mutilated body of the murdered man and hope that Sean doesn't remember the attack. I don't want him to know he has killed. There is nothing that can be done for this man, and it is my belief that this person's life was destined to be short. It is not important and, selfishly, I am in no mood to endure the endless guilt trip that would become our journey. It's going to be difficult enough as it is. I cover the bloodstains with an old tarpaulin and then try to rest as much as the howling will allow.

It's been a very long day and I wonder why it didn't kill me. Perhaps Sean still has some kind of free will. Is he is able to momentarily resist its strength, I wonder. I could have sworn I saw a flash of recognition in the eyes of the Sior-Mabuz. This realization drives me on as I become all-the-more determined to free Sean from his captor. Is it possible that Sean's feelings for my safety are stronger than the brute strength of the Sior-Mabuz? As night gets closer, I relax. The beast becomes quiet. It lays still and I see signs of Sean's reappearance. I take my jacket and put it over the both of us as I lie by his side. I remain as quiet as I do still. I relish the opportunity to get close to him. I push all thoughts of the grimy walls and filthy floors from my mind as I imagine we are together. I feel the warmth of his body next to mine and, as his heart rhythm returns to normal, I float in ecstasy as my thoughts transport us to a world a million miles away…

Chapter 3

I check my watch and realize we have very little time if we are to make it to the airport. I pull myself away, sit up and call to Sean. He wakes up immediately. I let myself believe he was secretly awake the whole time we lay together.

"Is it time to go?" he says rubbing his eyes. "There were people here…"

"Yes, you changed and they ran in fear." I must prevent him from finding out the truth. I scan the floors and see no sign of blood. His eyes follow mine. "I cannot see your shoe," I say in my effort to distract him from my mental search of the place.

"Was anyone hurt?" he says looking around. I fear he is aware on some level.

"Here it is," I say as I hand it to him. "Now hurry up, Sean."

"Destiel, did I hurt anyone?" he insists.

"No, you changed and they ran for their lives. They were in no hurry to stick around."

"Well, I guess you wouldn't be," he sniggers as he stands up and attempts to straighten his torn clothes. I am glad he is ignorant of the murder committed by the Sior-Mabuz. It would serve no purpose to tell him the truth, and we must make haste in any case.

We abandon the car close to the airport and dash as fast as we can. We have to make it, neither of us can keep going much longer but we must get there. We need to get Sean locked up once and for all. I am relieved when we reach the doors and get inside without drawing any attention to ourselves. I get us something to eat while Sean heads to the bathroom to try and make himself look presentable. We cannot risk being conspicuous.

I wait for him at the table with our food, time seems to have flown by quickly. We don't have much longer to wait now. I begin to eat and then I see him stroll back. He's done a good job of tending to his appearance. The cuts and bruises look less pronounced and, if anything, add a little more handsome ruggedness to his face. He looks great. He returns to the table and drinks. I prompt him to eat but he can barely manage a bite. He's very quiet and gloomy despite his trying to hide it. Sadly, I believe he has come to accept his fate.

We sleep through the majority of the journey on the plane, only opening our eyes briefly to eat or check the time. I am grateful for the flight as I know I will need all my energy when we get to Scotland. It feels nice to be together and I can't help but wonder how he feels about me. I'm sure he was already awake earlier, and I know that thing could've killed me but he stopped it. He's a good friend to me but how far does that go, it has to be more. It just has to be.

"Will you get off me," he says as I rest my head on his shoulder, and then I know that all thoughts of love are just a silly fantasy. I turn away from him and doze until it is time to endure the next leg of our mission.

We strenuously barge our way through the bustle of Glasgow Airport. We have to get outside and steal a car as quickly as possible in order to get to the industrial estate. We will stay there until we are able to make the journey to Hielan De'il Stravaig Castle. People are staring at us but it is a necessity we hurry. I pray we are not detained in any way. I would never have envisioned the amount of barrier stops before we could get a clear run towards the door, and even then the crowd seems to hinder us at every opportunity.

Once we get outside, we keep going until we come to busy main road. He stops and looks around before making off towards the city centre. I call to him as I know there will be far too many people in that direction.

"This way, Sean," I yell as I point to the subway which takes us beneath the busy road. He swiftly turns around and I see him hurtling towards me. He seems so panicky, it's the first time I have seen him so out of control. He is usually so calm and collected, nothing fazes him. We hurry and once inside the tunnel we take a breather. Neither of us can go on, and if we don't stop we will fall before we get anywhere near where we need to be. I sit on the floor whilst Sean leans against the wall. We pant furiously until we catch our breath.

"I can't keep going, Dest," he says urgently. I can see from his pale complexion that the Sior-Mabuz is wearing him down. He is losing his battle for life. I cannot bear it. I do not know how much longer Sean will live and I had not anticipated how soon the trauma would impact his health to such an extent. How stupid I have been. Of course it will kill him. I ponder for a moment that this might be a blessing, but then I remember our sacred texts about death and ascension. A soul's energy cannot be diffused without total overall cell death and disintegration, and this will not happen to Sean. The creature will act as a barrier to the dispersal of his energy. I begin to panic. His future situation is possibly a fate worse than death. I stand up and approach him.

"You have to keep going," I order him as menacingly as I can. "You are the only thing standing between this thing and a million deaths."

"Stop with the drama, Dest. I just don't give a shit anymore," he laughs weakly, and I realize the Sior-Mabuz is beginning to harden his heart. This is the same Sean who would normally trade his own life for the lowliest person alive.

"Sean, this isn't you talking, you don't mean this. Don't let it win." I get close to him. "You are the most compassionate person I've ever met."

"Yeah right," he says as he rests his hand against my arm to stop himself from falling over. I hold tight, steadying him as he glances shyly towards me before gazing to the ground. He doesn't mean a word of this. It's all talk, he would never put his own desires before others. "We don't have much time," he says quietly.

"I won't let it change you, Sean," I say as I put my arm around him. He lifts his head and I see tears in his eyes. I feel his body close to me, his warmth envelops me and I am overcome with love for him. He holds me tighter and presses himself into me. I close my eyes and then my mouth meets his. His lips are full and soft and my heart pounds as we kiss. I feel his fingers run through my hair and I tingle all over as I pass my hand up his over his shoulder and cup his beautiful face. All I can think is that he loves me, Sean loves me…

Then, suddenly, he breaks free from my arms and runs off. I call after him but he is soon out of sight. I follow him and come up on the other side of the road but he is completely out of view. I don't know what to do and curse myself for letting something so stupid happen. I fear for the lives of the people of this city, and for my own destiny. I know I cannot give in to my temptation or I will not be allowed my Timeship back. It is forbidden for me to have a relationship in any other time period but my own, in case a person is conceived and the whole planet be altered as a result. It is abhorrent to allow one's own desires to change the destiny of the world, although some have done it. This is one of the most troubling aspects of time travel. We are not lawfully allowed a life beyond righting wrongs and fighting the war that never ends. If only I did not possess the powers I do, I would never have been assigned this job... but then, I would never have met Sean. Despite everything, I am grateful I know him.

The authorities are aware of my feelings for someone here but they do not know with whom I am infatuated. If they did, Sean would surely be brought into the future and executed. The fact I am attached to a guy is even worse than if I were to have gotten involved with a woman. It is punishable by death. We obey one religion and this kind of relationship has been forbidden by God. The Church made it illegal three hundred years before I was born. We are assigned partners in life and so this kind of relationship is not heard of where I come from. I cannot allow myself to become weak in this matter ever again. If I continue to display signs of romantic attachment when I plug into the primary construct, I will be held prisoner in this very year forevermore. I have managed to overcome some of the frequency outputs, such as location within location and constant thought monitoring, but I am yet to control my emotional output enough to be completely free. I am one of the lucky ones that I have come so far towards some kind of true existence. There is one thing I do know, amongst all things; if I were to take my romantic attachment towards Sean to the point of us being lovers, I would no longer be able to hide it and would, at the very least, be disowned. If I ever attempted to return home, I would be sentenced to death. I am homesick. Is love worth giving up everything for? Especially when the person you love does not return your feelings? I fear I have taken advantage of Sean's weakness and now I must find him and get him locked up in Hielan De'il Stravaig Castle, where he now belongs.

I roam the city in search of him and barely two hours pass by when I come across a decapitated body. The crowds gather and the police are doing what they can to keep order but the panic has already set in. It seems everyone has become aware of this demonic creature, some have even seen its true form. I listen carefully, tuning out all background noise in order to listen only for words that matter. From what I can make out, amongst the chatter of the crowds, is that it has killed several people. The trail seems to revolve around the outer edge of the city. There's nothing I can do but keep looking in the hope I find it and, if I don't, I will wait until nightfall, when the Sior-Mabuz becomes Sean once again. I know he will seek refuge in a place he can restrain himself.

I head to the town centre, I suspect this thing will attempt to ingratiate itself where there are many females to choose from. It will have gained enough energy from the murders to maintain Sean's appearance. I will have the best chance of finding it there. It will be in Sean's form as it goes about its business unnoticed. Perhaps under these circumstances I will have a chance to stun and hold it if it is unsuspecting of my presence. How I will then get it to safety, I do not know but I hope instinct will take over at this point.

I am unlucky. I do not locate it before nightfall. I have let the people of this city down and I have failed Sean. How terrible he must feel and it is my fault. I should have protected him but instead I left him open to injury and soul-damaging emotional torture. My feelings turn to apathy as I acknowledge that I am incomplete in my ability to control a situation at its most crucial point. I feel utterly useless. I get myself a pastry and a cup of soup from a street vendor. I then sit on a bench outside the railway station and keep a lookout for Sean. I know he is unlikely to use such a mode of transport but I have nothing left but hope. He will attempt to get as far away from as many people as possible and hide himself. I believe it is wishful thinking on my part that he might show up, but there is something inside me stirring and I feel he might be near. I decide to rest for a time, my legs feel like lead. I have been running all day. My whole body is weary and my heart aches for Sean's return.

As I understand it, the Sior-Mabuz killed ninety two people by sundown. There are police helicopters everywhere. The whole city is in a state of panic. I must now attempt to locate Sean, but first I must eat and refresh my will to hunt. I must come to terms with my failure and compose myself. I will not be of assistance in this whole mess if I cannot forge ahead with a positive mind-set. I can't imagine how Sean is now feeling, he is out there - cold, alone and lost. He may remember the murders. Although, he may have been asleep and oblivious through the majority of the rampage. One thing is for sure, he will know that many people have died. He will soon grasp that slaughter on this scale could have only been committed by the Sior-Mabuz. I wonder if he has been captured. I decide to make this my first point of search. I will scour the police stations first. If Sean has been contained somehow, it will be because the Sior-Mabuz has suffered an injury, leaving it vulnerable. If this is so, then the creature will replenish itself overnight and then extinguish the life of anyone holding it captive. It *will* make its escape from custody. Only the dungeon of Hielan De'il Stravaig Castle, can hold the beast.

I take the last glug of my soup before wearily dragging myself to my feet. I turn to glance at the clock, and that is when I see Sean to my side. I am startled at first and then overwhelmed with relief. He is dirty, although his clothes have changed. He is wearing blue jeans, a blue shirt, and is holding a woollen hat. I guess they have been removed from a victim but I hold out hope they have merely been stolen.

I dash towards him and, to my surprise, he hugs me tightly. I notice him shivering and immediately remove my coat and wrap it around his shoulders before holding him again. We remain locked together and I know he is desperately wiping his eyes as leans over my shoulder. I allow him to compose himself before attempting to talk to him.

"I'm sorry, Dest, I shouldn't have run off like that. I just can't do that with *you*. It doesn't feel right and…"

"Its okay, Sean," I say quietly as I move away from him. "I'm sorry too. It was a mistake we need to forget." I smile and he nods. I can tell he is unburdened by the decision to put it behind us. "How are you?" I ask. It's a stupid question given the circumstances, and I instantly regret my foolish words.

"I've killed people, Dest."

"No, Sean. The Sior-Mabuz has killed people," I say softly as I try and pacify his guilt.

"Yeah because of me," he moans childishly.

"Listen to me, Sean, you have saved far more people than you have ever harmed. Your heroism is legendary. If there had been more like you, there never would have been a war to start with."

"People still died…"

"You've got to pull yourself together if we're going to see this through. In the future people still speak your name in recognition of your bravery."

"Really?" he asks, his face lighting up. "It doesn't matter, the reputation ends now," he says. He is caught up in his own self-loathing once again. I find it slightly annoying. We have more pressing things to attend to.

"Sean," I snap angrily as I hold him by the collar. "What you need to do, what you *will* do, when you commit yourself to the dungeon of Hielan De'il Stravaig forever, is payment enough for this *one* mistake. Now, let's make haste."

I see this has shocked some perspective into his troubled mind. I pull my hand away from his neck. I wish I hadn't needed to do that to him but sometimes the end justify the means. He takes a deep breath and we finally get moving. We head out of the city centre as fast as possible. It doesn't take long before we find ourselves in some side streets and I feel slightly better to be out of the sight of passers-by. We soon come up on a desolate lane. There is no one around and so we take a car. We have no choice, we cannot risk delay. By my reckoning we need four hours to get to the small island of Hielan De'il Stravaig. We cannot drive fast as we must not risk drawing attention to ourselves. I hope the car owner does not notice his vehicle is missing until morning. We set off. I allow Sean to drive as I believe the distraction will be good for him.

"Sean, I need to make a call," I say as I consider our arrival. I dial the number and am relieved to have reached a friendly voice. I arrange a time with Connell, the Laird of the castle, and he assures me he will be there waiting with a boat for the last stint of our journey. Neither of us will have the strength to make the swim, and I don't relish the thought of reaching the castle soaked through.

"Who *is* that?" Sean asks appearing worried. "I didn't know there were people there."

"There isn't. The castle itself is empty and has been for many, many years, but for the Sior-Mabuz."

"Who was that then?"

"There is a man named Connell Balliol. He is the Laird - he owns the island and land around it. The

47

property has been in his family for centuries. His clan were instrumental in the capture and containment of the creature when it first became known to us. The secret has continued through their family line until this very day."

"How do you know he didn't free it? Maybe he…"

"Because I just read his thoughts. This man has never even seen the Sior-Mabuz. He assists only in that he keeps an eye on the castle and maintains it for us. He does not enter the dungeon. This would be stupid of him."

"Maybe he did. Maybe he couldn't help himself and that's how it got out."

"If he had done, he would not be talking to me because he would be dead. He is not lying to us, he is unaware of how it escaped. Sean, we are lucky to have his help. Without his protection and assistance, we would have nowhere to contain this thing."

"You mean *me*, don't you?"

"Yes."

"How long will you stay there with me?"

"There are four rooms inside the castle, where there is liveable accommodation for such emergencies. I will chain you, ensure you are secure, rest and be on my way within a couple of days." I look to see Sean swallow hard. This is truly awful, and I see his will to live become that much less. He says nothing for the remainder of the journey.

We get close and I indicate where we are to go. He follows my instructions and we come up on the edge of the Loch. We have no option but to roll the car into it. We watch as it careers down the steep bank, drops into the water and then sinks.

"I hope he didn't need that to get to work tomorrow," Sean says with a chuckle. I smile and am comforted that he is still able to find his sense of humour. We start off on the mile long walk to the boat ramp. From there we will take the boat which will get us to the castle of Hielan De'il Stravaig.

"I need you, Dest," he says as he stumbles and reaches out for my arm. "I can't make it any further without you." He grasps me and I cling to his arm as I hold him up. I latch onto him like my life depends on it and we struggle on as if we are locked into one another.

"Not much farther, Sean, you can do it. You've come this far, just hold on and we'll do this together." I feel his pull come harder on me as he musters the strength he needs to endure the pain he undoubtedly feels. I consider how much it must hurt to have that thing inside. I'm not sure I could take it. He has shown little complaint for his own suffering. The pain of others causes so much more torment to him. He will never become one with this monster. His altruism and strength of character is unlike any I have ever met. I am in awe of Sean's spirit, and this only makes what I have to do to him all the tougher.

When we arrive, we see a shimmering light in the small hut.

"Hang on, Dest, how do we know it's safe?" Sean says straightening up sharply.

"It's safe," I reassure him as we push on towards the light. I ache all over but am relieved as we approach and see Connell waiting for us. Finally, our journey is almost over. We quietly approach the man, although there is nobody around for miles who would hear us.

"Hi, Connell, thanks for this. It's appreciated."

"It's good to see you again, Destiel," he replies. "I've prepared a room and lit a fire for you as well," he says with a friendly smile, which soon fades to a frown as his gaze turns towards Sean.

"This the monster? Ugly or what," he says as he recoils slightly in alarm.

"Yeah… well… you wanna see me in the morning, Pal," Sean replies.

"Sean," I snap. "This isn't funny."

"Hold on a minute. Tell him that, he started it," Sean replies. I look towards Connell to find him glaring at Sean. I swiftly turn my attention to the boat.

"You've done great here, Connell," I say in an effort to defuse the awkward tension of Sean's misplaced humour.

"Yeah, thanks, man. Really appreciate your help," Sean says as he holds his hand out to thank Connell with a handshake. Connell ignores his hand gesture.

"Let's just get on with it," the Laird replies. He is displeased and I understand that it is not easy keeping this secret, let alone standing about half the night in the bitter cold.

"No problem," Sean says with forced cheer. "Come on, Destiel, let's get going," he says as he gets into the boat and plonks himself down. I linger ashore for a moment longer to thank Connell once again. I reassure him there will not be another escape. I then watch him walk away before clambering aboard the boat myself.

I see that Sean is about to fall asleep and I have no desire to keep him from rest, and so I pick up an oar and begin to row us towards the castle. My heart is heavy as I consider the terrible truth, Sean will soon be leaving my life forever.

Chapter 4

I carry him inside when we arrive, and gently lay him on the couch. I then push it towards the crackling fire and let him sleep. A person could be forgiven for believing they are in a luxurious old castle resort. I am surprised to see these rooms taken care of so well. Everything a person could need has been thought of and provided for. Connell must have been here regularly to maintain it to such a high standard. It crosses my mind that this is unusual. It had always been fairly lightly provisioned on the occasions I had needed its use in the past. There is no indication that outside of these rooms is an abandoned old castle with a dank, dark dungeon beneath. I can find no sense in Connell going to so much trouble. I ponder this for a few moments before deciding he is either a very considerate person or he selfishly envisioned that he may have needed to use the accommodation himself, should we ever require his help with anything.

I hurt for Sean and I am so sad he will spend his days locked within the decrepit pit downstairs. I sit for a time and watch him sleep. He is peaceful and it is impossible for me to believe that such a monster could exist behind such an angelic face. I creep near to him as I remember our kiss. I go as close as I can without waking him. I feel his breath against my face and I long for his touch. I am tempted to put my lips to his so I can taste him just one more time, but I do not. I force myself away. I have to remain practical. It's not long before I will be far away. I can return to my duties and resume my confinement within this time zone until I have detached from my feelings. It won't be easy but I have a job to do, an important one. I will work hard to show I am in control once again. This way, I will prove myself worthy of being the Wayfarer I am, and am destined to be. My duty is to put right the wrongs of the past to ensure the survival of humanity. I will return home when I am ready, and once again I will be the pilot of my own destiny. These feelings of lust will fade over time. Sadly, I know that my guilt over Sean's incarceration will not.

I head to the kitchen to find Connell has provided well. I begin to make dinner for Sean. I try as best I can to deliver something nourishing but, without culinary expertise, the best I can manage is a cooked breakfast. I get to work. I know there isn't much time left, and I would like to say a proper goodbye.

It isn't long before I have prepared an adequate meal. It would appear that Connell is quite fond of frying because much of the food afforded to us needs to be cooked in such a way. I wonder if this man is healthy, it would seem from his food selection that he is not.

My thoughts are interrupted when I hear a voice behind me. I am startled and abruptly drop my pan on the floor, spilling its contents as I do so.

"This looks, great, Dest, I'm starving," Sean gasps. "This Connell guy certainly knows how to look after guests." He rubs his stomach eagerly and all but drools.

"I am glad you approve, Sean," I say as I bend over, scrape what I can back inside, and pick up my pan. I wonder why he feels hungry. He hardly ate anything at all today. The Sior-Mabuz does not require food, this I know for sure.

"Why so jumpy, Dest, not scared of me are you?" he says. I look up and narrow my eyes in disapproval. "You sure know how to rustle up a fry-up though. Don't worry, I'll risk it," he says looking at my sausage. I sigh as I pick it up off the floor and put it on his plate.

"Not like I have to worry about food poisoning is it?" he laughs.

"I didn't expect you to wake up so soon," I say, feeling concerned. He seems energised but we still have a couple of hours before sunrise. I look at him closely, inspecting for signs of the creature surfacing.

"It's *me*," he says as he takes his plate and sits at the table. I watch as he bolts his meal. He is famished and I wonder when he last ate. Perhaps his lack of food has made him weaker. I hope this is the reason he appears ill and not because he is losing vitality. I do not want him to die, and then my mind drifts… I decide that I will never stop looking for a way out of this. If he can stay alive in this condition, I will not give up on him. He is fighting to remain himself even against the mighty will of this creature. I must not lose sight of the fact that I am the only one who can save him from this plight. Even if he does die in the process of being saved, at least I will have freed his soul from this hell. If I can just rest, I can think better. There must be something I can do, someway, somehow. I will harness my knowledge of this creature and defeat it. I will do it for *him*.

We talk for a time about general stuff, neither of us wanting to think about the inevitable imprisonment which is drawing ever closer by the second. I keep a sneaky eye on the clock, I cannot let him change before he is restrained. There is still time and I allow myself to enjoy his company for a while - what can it hurt now. So what if I let myself fall a little deeper in love… for just one last night… before I say goodbye. I will reach deep inside my chest when morning comes and pull my own heart out if it means I can feel this way right now.

We laugh and talk as if it were old times again, just like in those years before all this happened and we were friends. Way back before my feelings were discovered, in a time when I was merely happy to be around him. I now love him more than ever before. I worship him, and I know I will never feel the same about another living soul. How could this have happened to me? All I ever wanted to do was to use the gift bestowed on me and serve my civilization. It was my dream since I was a boy, and here I am on verge of throwing it all away for the smallest chance of reciprocal love. But I know, deep down, that he doesn't feel the same way for me. I would do it, I would walk away from everything just for him, even if all we ever had together was one day. If he loved me for just one day, one day in a whole lifetime that would be enough, but I know I am chasing crayon rainbows. I must fight against these feelings and I know that I must leave this place in order to banish them from my heart.

After the meal, Sean stands up and grins. I wonder what he is thinking, he is beginning to act strangely. Perhaps he is frightened of what is to come.

"Well, come on then, you gonna show me around my new home?" he asks. I hesitate as I look at the clock. "Stop dithering, Dest, we have hours yet. As you said yourself, it gets lighter later here." He smiles and I am reminded that the sun does rise much later, especially this far up the country, and so I agree to the tour. The first room he walks into is the one which has been prepared for me to sleep in. "Well, this a bit rough, I hope you manage to get some shuteye in this dump," he says as he lays his eyes on the sumptuous four-poster bed. I notice the plush pile of the carpets and the splendid décor of the room which will be my resting place tonight. The shame overwhelms me.

"I did not envision such opulence," I say immediately.

"Wanna trade?" he says grinning as he takes a glance out of the window and his face morphs into an expression of horror. I guess he is seeing the vast body of water laid out before him. The welcoming twinkles of the town in the distance are a cruel reminder of his looming isolation.

"Let's take a look around the rest of the castle," I say in order to distract him from his trepidation. Solitary confinement - that's what he was thinking. I heard his mind say it. I cannot usually read Sean's thoughts in such a way. Perhaps it's because his guard is so low. I preferred it when I couldn't sense his brainwaves. It might be selfish of me but I find it intolerable to know his fear.

We take a walk slowly around, careful not to fall. The castle is very cold and dark. The torches we have are not nearly bright enough for such blackness. We go from room to room and mingle amongst the imaginary spectres who haunt these walls. Dark figures move and twist forebodingly wherever we walk. I feel the wrath in their cold stares. Their sinister whispers falling like chalk dust onto blank slates, our minds rearranging the specks into screaming words of torment. The water drips and the small animals scurry around us as we tread cautiously on, knowing the basement beckons. I do not dare mention it, and I cannot stand to think of this horror. It's almost as if the darkness ahead foreshadows the darkness to come. The idea of the man I love being trapped here forever is too much to stand. I pull Sean by the arm as I suggest we go back, but he insists we continue on. We don't get much further into our tour when Sean stops and turns to me. He holds my shoulder and I already know what he will say before he has even begun.

"Let's just go there now. I want to see it," he says. I know he means the dungeon. I reluctantly agree, he has a right to familiarise himself with his fate. It's not my place to stand in his way. We silently make our way there. I'm filled with anguish as I hear the anxiety in his breath as we descend the castle staircase. We reach the trap door. It's stiff and so we tug it together until it comes, at which point, we both fall to the floor under its weight. Sean scrambles up and shines his torch into the dungeon. He then tiptoes down the steps until he gets to another two doors. "Welcome to eternity," he announces. I follow after him and watch as he opens the door to the next flight of steps and continues on his way to the dark pit. Once we are there, we look around and manage to see that the restraints that held the creature have quite possibly deteriorated enough to have been broken by its strength. "Could've maintained this better, Dest," he says as he shines his torch in my face.

"I'm sorry, Sean," I say as I am overcome with remorse. He laughs.

"I'm kidding. None of this is your fault, Destiel. I mean it," he says as he taps my arm in an effort to console me. The glare from his torch flashes around and then settles on the exit. "Let's get out of here. I'm not spending any more time than I have to in this hole."

We head back to the cosy living quarters and I make us both a mug of cocoa. When I return to the sitting room, Sean is stood at the window. I set our drinks down on the table. I just don't know what to say to him. I imagine what is running through his mind as I lie back on one of the couches. It's warm and serene but I sense Sean is troubled, except... it doesn't appear to be his impending doom which is frustrating him. I ask him what's wrong.

"Uh, what do you think?" he says turning to face me as he raises his eyebrows.

"There's something else, Sean," I say. "I feel it." I watch as he looks away and shrugs. I decide not to push it.

"Your drink is getting cold, Sean. It will warm you," I say as I put my hands behind my head. I close my eyes for a moment, only to open them again to find he is knelt in front of me. His eyes are locked hard onto my own. We gaze at each other. Everything that has happened just falls away as I am captured in the moment, mesmerised by his hazy stare.

"Destiel, I'm sorry about what happened in Glasgow," he says.

"Sean, I don't hold you responsible I..."

"No, for what happened in the subway." I am shocked he has so blatantly brought up our passionate encounter.

"There is no need for an apology, Sean."

"I can't pretend anymore. I have to be honest with you. My feelings for you have grown. I have always thought a lot of you but something has changed and… well… I now have some sort of deeper attraction to you."

"Sean, this is because you are not yourself," I say reassuringly. "Your own mind and desires will return, should we ever manage to find a way to free you."

"That's not going to happen though is it? Besides, I know what I feel. It's nothing to do with that thing being inside me. It's *you*. I can't live without you near me. You make everything okay. I feel safe when you're around. I always have but something is different. It's as if we are connected somehow and designed to depend on each other."

"This is fear of loneliness talking, Sean."

"It's not. Damn it, Dest," he says as he pushes his hands up into his hair in apparent frustration at my logical explanation. I'm not about to jump on you, don't panic," he scoffs. He turns to pull away and I grab his arm. Maybe I'm taking advantage of his vulnerable position but I can't help myself. I don't care whether this is right or wrong. I want him.

"I love you, Sean," I say softly as he returns his gaze to me.

"Well there's no need to go that far," he says as he attempts to move away again and I pull him back to me. He weakens and allows my invitation. He comes in closer, until his face is right before mine. "I love you, Sean," I repeat. "I always have, you're everything to me." He stares at me intensely for a moment, and then our lips come together as he kisses me. My body fills with desire, and I can keep my feelings hidden no longer as I throw off the shackles of self-control. I slide my hand up inside the back of his shirt and brush my fingers across his soft skin. He pulls away from me again and, sensing my yearning to touch him, yanks his top up over his head before laying down beside me. We kiss again and I revel in our closeness as I stroke him. My whole life melts away, all my old hopes and dreams gone, traded for the love of Sean. I feel him unfasten my shirt buttons and my heart pounds as I will him to touch me. He pushes my clothes aside and I lie back as he tenderly kisses my chest and softly runs his fingers over my skin. My whole body trembles with desire for him. I have never wanted anyone more and I feel our togetherness completes me

Then, as quickly as it came, it is over as he slides away from me. I make a grab for him with the intention of pulling him back and never letting him go.

"I have to get downstairs," he says as he stands up. I reach out and take his hand but he slips it from me.

"I need you," I say, desperately. "Be with me."

"You know that's not possible." He looks to the ground and I pull myself together. "It's time, Dest. I gotta go down."

"I know," I say quietly as I get up and prepare myself for what is to come.

We make for the door, my hands tremble as I turn the handle.

"You ready?" I ask. He blinks hard and then smiles sweetly as he gives me the thumbs up. "Come on," I say taking his hand as we leave the comfort of the room. The cold hits us hard and we hurry to the stairs. As usual, time is very much against us. If only we could have had a few more moments together. We rush down to the ground floor. He needs to be chained as soon as possible before the thing inside is awoken by the morning sun. We get to the bottom and I release my grip, only to see him walk the wrong way. I quickly grab him once more and lead him to the dungeon. Why, oh why, have I got to be the one to do this to him? I scream inside as we set foot in the damp and dismal cavern. Once inside, he thrusts himself at the wall and wraps the new chains and cuffs around himself. His self-restraint is amazing and I don't know where he finds the courage to go through with this. I shake as I attempt to fasten the cuffs into place. I can see he has begun to change form, and my mind is party to the fight going on inside his head as he struggles against the creature. His willpower is like none I have ever encountered. My brow sweats as I manage to close the last clasp and pull away from Sean just before he mutates. I fall to the floor and witness the thing's anguish as it realizes it is once again imprisoned in the dungeon of Hielan De'il Stravaig.

"You will never leave this filthy pit again," I say to it as I turn and ascend the steps of the dungeon. I cannot bear to turn around before I leave. Once out, I lock the dungeon and return upstairs, to where I take to my bed and weep like an infant. "Sean, I need you," I whisper and then I scream his name over and over until I can scream no more. I then lie shivering as I sob myself to sleep.

Chapter 5

It's early evening when I awake with a start. I am dripping with sweat. At first, it would be easy to believe all this could all be a terrible nightmare, and then reality sets in. My first thought is for poor Sean, locked downstairs. He will be himself by now. He's probably very cold and very lonely, how will he ever come through this. I wonder if he will be hungry but then I remember that he no longer needs food, although his mind may yearn for it. I know it is not necessary anymore, as is breathing, or any other human need. I wonder whether he has given himself over to the beast and died. I should leave this place. I will come back when I find a cure for this sickness. I get myself together and head from the room to the hall. I catch my breath as I tread gingerly through the castle. I hear no sound. I want to go and rescue him but I know it is not possible. I should chance it and take one more peek at his handsome face, but my nerve fails me as I fear this last image would only haunt me for the rest of my days. I approach the dungeon door and shine my light on it. Still locked firm. I long to call down to him but I resist.

"Goodbye, Sean," I whisper before walking away from the door. I make my exit quickly, but as soon as I reach the boat, I stop dead in my tracks. I am overcome with sorrow and, as I sit on a rock and look towards where my Sean is imprisoned, I feel a chill run through me. I raise my voice and call that I am sorry, that I should have been a better friend. I wonder if he somehow hears me, or if my thoughts are strong enough to reach his mind. Please be so, I hope.

I need to move but my body won't let me. I push myself up and then slump back down. It's no use, I can't go on without him. I clear my mind and then set it firmly to thoughts of my return home. It seems to work, my trembling stops and I am able to find my footing to stand, eventually getting to my feet. I place one foot inside the boat and then remove it again. I urge my body to get into the vessel, but it will not move. "Get into the boat," I order myself, but still I linger. I turn around, follow my heart, and head back to the castle.

All is quiet when I open the door of the basement. I wonder if Sean is dead. I hope he is just sleeping. I creep down the steps and steadily approach the shackles. It's very dark but I can make out a chain. I raise my torch, fearing what I might see, and then I catch movement. The light settles on his glistening green eyes, and he squints as he raises his hand to his face as a shield.

"Do you mind?" he says, and I quickly avert the light from his gaze. "What you doing here, Dest?" he sighs regretfully. "You shouldn't have come here."

"You're okay?" I say, relieved to hear him speaking to me. I rush to him and fling my arms around him.

"What did you expect? I'm not about to roll over and die the first night am I?"

"I can't leave you, Sean."

"Damn it, Dest, you have to. Now turn around and walk away, Destiel." He falls silent and I stand firm. "Go," he shouts.

"No!" I retaliate loudly.

"No?" He sighs deeply in disbelief. "You have to."

"I can't, I won't. I won't leave you here, Sean." I shake with determination as I confront him. I resolve to stand by my decision no matter what. I hear him sigh again, more loudly this time. I know he will not beat me on this matter.

"Well, you might wanna undo these things then," he says, rattling his chains. I smile. I don't know what will happen from here, but I do know I have just made the decision to leave behind everything that ever mattered in my life. I know now that I can never return home to my own time. I have made this choice for him, for Sean, for the love of Sean.

We leave the dungeon. We now have all night together before he must be returned to lockdown. We know we must decide how we can deal with this predicament but, for now, we decide to go outside and take a walk, to breathe some fresh air and take a break from this awful turmoil. We collect some warm clothing from the wardrobe upstairs and head straight outside.

The crisp air cuts into us immediately. I hadn't noticed it before but now it enters my lungs like ice. I am hardened to it though, it washes over me and I don't mind. I have a warm, glowing spark inside my chest, ready to light a fire inside me, and for the first time in my life, I know what true love is.

The evening moon is bright and the water laps lightly at the shore. The sounds are like music to my soul. I feel drunk on the moment. I can imagine nowhere better to be right now. I turn to Sean, his face glistens in the moonlight and, as he smiles, I slip my hand in his. He accepts my gesture and we walk together as we explore the evening garden. This must be what it feels like to be a teenager on a first date.

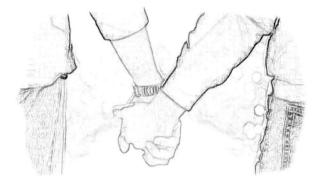

We are quiet at first but it isn't awkward. We are both so relieved to be out of that place that we welcome the silence between us. My mind drifts to the horror of the dungeon and I immediately push it out. I will not let it come between us on this special night. The creature will not win.

"This place has a certain charm to it," I say, hoping to distract myself from my own thoughts of the castle prison.

"That's not the place, Dest," he laughs. "That's my scintillating company. I'm irresistible, admit it."

"I do admit it," I say as I turn and pull him towards me. He wraps his arms around my waist and our bodies become close. I hold his face. "I would do anything for you," I tell him.

"Anything?" he smiles cheekily.

"*Anything*," I reply as I look coyly into his eyes. He moves his head up close to me. I think is going to kiss me and then he whispers in my ear.

"How about one of those mean breakfasts of yours then?" he says. I laugh and we turn around and walk back to the castle, running for the last few steps as we feel a light sprinkle of rain begin to come down.

When we arrive back I head to the kitchen while Sean lights a fire for us to keep warm by. I can hear the rain has picked up and I am grateful that we came back when we did. I cook an extra special meal for Sean, although I wonder what we will do for food from now on as rations will begin to run low very soon. Connell has provided for a few days at most and we could be here forever. I will have to go into the town, which is quite some distance. Something will need to be done. I will need to get my hands on a car.

I set the table and call to Sean, who is now in the bedroom after having gone for a shower. I place our meal on the table and wait for him for him to arrive, which he does a couple of minutes later. He is wearing a brown checked shirt and canvass trousers, which he must have found in the wardrobe. He looks different, his hair has fallen forward slightly, where it hasn't been combed back in the usual style. It frames his face and he looks cuter than ever.

"What?" he laughs. "There's not that much choice in there," he says looking down at his clothes. "I look like a farmer."

"It's not that, Sean," I smile. "I'm just so glad you're okay and that you're here with me... and... you look great."

"So does this," he says, gaping wide-eyed at his plate of food before devouring his first mouthful.

"Sean, we will need more food," I say as casually as I can. I do not want to spoil the evening but this is a fact. He stops chewing and stares at me.

"I will stop eating," he says. "I can survive without food but you can't."

"You need your strength," I say forcefully. "That thing is robbing your energy stock every day. How long will you keep your own appearance if you have no fuel?

How long before your body is burned up by that thing? I won't let it feed off you until you die. Also, I think that the food might be keeping it in check a little. That thing does not work well with food inside it. You need to keep eating."

"This is all my fault, I'm sorry, Destiel."

"This is no one's fault, Sean. It's okay, I will get food tomorrow. I'll go to the town. It will take me nearly all day but it needs to be done."

"Can't you get a supermarket home delivery?" he says before shoving the last morsel of dinner into his mouth, leaning back and rubbing his stomach with a look of satisfaction.

"No."

"Well, what about that Connell guy then, can't he bring something? He'll do it for you, Dest. You two seemed pretty pally if you ask me." I had thought about this but I am reluctant to involve others and besides, he won't keep doing it.

"I don't want him to know I am still here, Sean."

"Why not? You ashamed of me?" Sean sniggers.

"Of course not," I reply quickly.

"It's my day job, isn't it?" he laughs. "You're embarrassed." I know he's joking, but I can't help but wonder whether he would have taken things this far between us had this horror not occurred. Perhaps he has taken leave of his senses. I so hope he truly cares for me and this isn't just a security blanket for him. I've given up my chance of ever returning home - for him. I will no longer be able to keep the truth from them. The Responder will pick up my thoughts and feelings. This love is just too strong to hide.

"I will see about purchasing a car," I say, and then I see him gesture to speak. "No, I will not steal one," I say firmly. "We have to be careful. It's fine, I will take care of it. Just you rest and look after yourself. Please, for me?" I say as I smile and place my hand on his. He grins and continues to eat from the bread basket. He is still hungry after eating so much. In light of the Sior-Mabuz requiring no food, I don't know whether to be glad or worried. I decide that it can only be a good thing.

"You know what, Dest, I'm almost grateful to the old Sior-mabs. It's because of him I'm here sharing this with you. I wouldn't want to be anywhere else right now," he says before shoving in another mouthful of bread and grinning. I'm taken aback. I've never heard him say anything so kind and sensitive. My stomach turns to excited jelly and my nerves kick in. I smile to myself as I eat my food. I know he is watching me.

When we are finished our meal, we head into the living room where I place a cushion on the floor and lie in front of the fire to keep warm. Sean looks around uneasily for a moment and then, to my surprise, kneels on the floor next to me.

"Can I join you there?" he asks and I nod. He lays down with me and rests his head on my chest. Within moments he is asleep and I enjoy the gentle rocking of his body against mine as he breathes deeply.

He smells perfect, he feels perfect and I know it is right to have him with me. I allow the roar of the rain crashing against the window to wash over me, and it floods me with calm. I am filled with a sense of contentment unlike anything I could ever have wished for... and it is all because I am able to say that Sean is mine. At last, he is mine.

"I love you," I whisper as I drift off to sleep, knowing that I have never been surer of anything.

Chapter 6

I am disappointed when we awake and realize we only have an hour before Sean must be confined to the basement. We walk silently there and I notice that, once again, he forgets the way. I wonder whether his demise is close, perhaps the inevitable cell death has begun. I know the creature needs energy to renew the host subject's appearance. I wonder whether physical appearance is the last thing to go, just simply because this is the thing that the Sior-Mabuz values most. It *is* the *only* reason it takes a body. We must discuss what we are to do, and very soon. I just can't lose him now… or ever!

When I arrive back upstairs, I decide to call Connell after all. The journey into the town is arduous and I am reluctant to leave Sean. I make believe that I am wary of leaving the creature. I explain that it seems to have gained strength from the murders and so I must wait until it weakens. He agrees that he will meet me later in the day with food supplies and other necessary items. I set my alarm for late afternoon and then get some sleep. I intend to spend every second I can with Sean awake. Even if he sleeps, I want to be aware of his presence and know he is safe. I miss him and fear that I will find him dead when I least suspect it.

I manage to sleep without problems, and awaken in plenty of time to paddle to the other side of the water to meet Connell. He has done well and has provided enough food to last us for some time. I thank him and reassure him I can contain the animal. He is convinced by my story but is unfazed by the potential escape of the beast. I suppose that a person can get used to anything when they are exposed to an idea for long enough. He would have known of the Sior-Mabuz for many years now and so has become accustomed to its presence. I do not enjoy lying and it does not come easy to me, but it has become a necessary evil over the years. Lying is forbidden where I come from. The God does not allow this sin, and is keen to punish the deceitful by death. I long for the day Sean and I can be honest and live as a real couple and be together for always.

When I arrive back I drop the bags on the floor and walk towards the dungeon trapdoor. I hear no sound. I wonder why it is so quiet, surely the dungeon is not completely soundproof. I wonder if the creature has become frail. Perhaps Sean is winning the battle of wills, and then I hear a raucous moan and know the thing is alive and well. I take the things and return upstairs where I put them away and ponder what would happen to Sean if the creature could be killed. How immortal can anything truly be? Although, even if it were to be slain, I am doubtful whether Sean would survive. It is not a risk I could ever take.

I think things out until I can think no more but still, I come up with no clue about how I can free Sean from the grip of evil. I try to stop thinking about the problem. The idea of getting it to swap hosts is biting at me and I know it is something just too dangerous to use. I need to forget it. I decide that my ideas will gel of their own accord and present me with better answer. If

I let my telepathic abilities take the reins for a time, then something will come to mind. I turn my attention to thoughts of Sean and a happier future away from this oppressive state. I daydream about what our life could be like together and it makes me yearn. It's all I want.

I can hardly wait for evening to arrive. I need to know he's safe and I long to look into those beautiful emerald eyes. I remember our kiss and I feel excited that I may get the chance to take it further. I'm not sure Sean is ready for such a big leap but perhaps one day we will become lovers in the way I pine for. In the meantime, I am content with the closeness we have created between us. I take a look outside. The light is dimming, it won't be long now. I prepare a meal for Sean and place it into the oven ready for when he arrives. I know he will be famished. When I am finished, I am pleasantly surprised to see it is time to go downstairs. I feel uneasy but I know he will not hurt me, he could have done so back in New York but chose not to. Even if I should ever go down to find him still in the form of the Sior-Mabuz, I do not fear that he will hurt me. I realize now that it was his escalating feelings for me that prevented the Sior-Mabuz from attacking me when it had a chance. Sean stopped it hurting me, and I know that if he hadn't then the creature would have killed me. Why couldn't he have discovered his feelings before now, so that we may have had a chance at normality? Then, it crosses my mind once again that Sean is not quite himself and it is insecurity that has triggered his desperate need to be loved at all costs. I know my own feelings and who I want, but is Sean really so sure? He has had many girlfriends in the past and this is another reason I am troubled.

I shove away my nagging doubts and make my way down to the dungeon. I shine my torch towards him to find him lying on the floor. I panic as I run to him, slumping down on the floor as I arrive beside him. I frantically feel his neck for a pulse, and then he wakes up.

"Hey, I might look like shit but I'm not quite dead yet," he says and I laugh. I have never been so thankful.

"No, but you stink," I say. "Come on, let's get you out of here." I help him get up and we negotiate our way up the steps together.

"What's it called again?" he asks on the way up. "You know, that thing I turn into."

"It's called the Sior-Mabuz, Sean."

"Yes, that's it. How could I forget," he says sarcastically. I wonder why he has forgotten but I guess it *is* pretty exhausting to the body to be thrashing about all day, even if you are unaware of it. I then wonder how much he is actually aware of, but I decide not to ask. It is better he focuses on something else.

Sean is ravenous and so we share our meal together immediately. He then goes for a shower whilst I wait anxiously for him to return. When he doesn't, I knock on the bedroom door and ask if he is okay, but he doesn't answer. I slowly open the door to find him lying asleep on the bed with a towel around his waist. I take a deep breath as I look at his body. My instinct is to lie with him but I am reluctant, not knowing his response. I turn to leave again when I hear him stir.

"Hey, don't go," he whispers. I freeze to the spot. "Come back, Dest. I need a hug, I really do," he says sweetly. I can't help myself, I turn around and smile. He holds his hand out to me and I try to resist the temptation but I am just too weak-willed.

I walk towards the bed, "You'll never know how much I've wanted to hear you say these things," I say to him. I take my top off and get on the bed next to him.

"Where's my hug then," he asks and I immediately grab him tight and hold him close to me. I hear his breathing quicken and my heart pounds. We stay like this for a few moments and then, gradually, I pull away. At which point he leans over me and gently kisses me... once... then twice. Then he looks up at me and smiles seductively. His eyes sparkles and I know that he is teasing me, and I like it.

I move forward and skim my mouth against his and we kiss again, slowly at first and then passionately as I press my lips hard onto his and our embrace deepens. I am so aroused to feel him pressed hard against me and I want him so badly that I cannot restrain myself. I twist him over and run my hands enthusiastically over his body. I curb myself, he deserves more than this. I begin to softly stoke him instead. I look up to see he has closed his eyes and so I run my lips gently over his body, starting at his chest and working my way down to his stomach. I cannot resist, I push open his towel to expose the rest of him. His skin glistens in the low light, and the smooth contours of his body make me ache. He is so beautiful and, as I continue to kiss his body, he becomes more breathy and aroused to my touch. He is everything I desire and I want to please him so much. I begin to touch him lightly and when he softly moans, I move in and continue to gently caress him with my mouth. I enjoy the sounds of his groans as he becomes more and more excited, and I do not stop until he is satisfied.

I am so happy I have been able to make him feel special. I am dizzy with adoration as I return to his arms, where we cuddle until he sleeps. I do not sleep. I am buzzing from our closeness and I want nothing more than to lay next to him and hold him whilst he is so peaceful and vulnerable.

A few hours have passed by when he wakes up. He kisses me and I smile as I run my hand through his hair. He asks me if I am okay and I nod. I have begun to feel a little melancholy but I do my best to appear relaxed.

"What's up, Dest, do you regret what happened?" he whispers sadly.

"No!" I say as I turn to him, horrified he would think such a thing. "I love you, more than anything."

"What is it then? I know something is wrong. Is it just this whole monster thing?"

"Not just, Sean… but…"

"It's okay, Dest, I'm fine. I feel it gnawing at my insides from time to time but I have you and that makes it okay." He smiles with unease as if suddenly becoming aware of something. "Is that it? You're leaving aren't you?" He sits up and holds his head and I reach out and put my hand on his shoulder.

"I will never leave you. No matter what," I tell him and I think he understands that I mean it.

"Then everything is good," he says. He is smiling as if we don't have a care in the world. He is in complete denial, or perhaps he is simply prepared to give in. This is so unlike him. My memory jolts me back to July 2nd 2028, the very first day I ever saw him. I'd heard of him, of course, but he was nothing like I had expected. I'd always imagined him to be some fine upstanding paragon of virtue. The sort of person who always does things by the book, a - boring but gets the job done – type. He wasn't, he was just a man doing what he could to survive, using whatever means necessary to defeat the enemy. But there was something else too, there was a charisma about him that made you believe in him. People do whatever he asks of them, without question. He has a way of talking a person round to his way of thinking and, no matter how the odds are stacked, he comes through, time and time again. He's not the ideal candidate and his methods aren't always practical, but he is the ideal choice. If he hadn't done what he did, there would be no future. But now, the fighter in him is gone, it's as if he's washed up and the war is over for him. This isn't him talking, he would never stop fighting that thing inside him. If he can bring peace to a twenty year conflict, why can't he bring it to himself? He despises the machines, everything about them, and now he seems to be throwing it all in. He is being overwritten by this creature's programming. I can't let this happen. I will not let it change him.

"No, it's not, Sean," I say loudly, hoping to shock him back into reality. "Everything is *not* good."

"What?" he says, turning swiftly at me. I see the contempt in his eyes. He is angry with me.

"I'm sorry," I say as I sit up beside him. "I can't lose you, not now. We have to talk about this, we can't just..."

"Right," he says sighing heavily. "Can't we just enjoy what we've got for a minute," he says. I know he is becoming even more agitated and I don't want to cause him distress but it has to be talked about.

"Sean, you don't know what it's like for me wondering whether I'll arrive in the basement to find your lifeless corpse wrapped around that disgusting

81

brute. It *will* happen and I cannot bear it. I just can't," I say raising my voice slightly. He gets out of bed and dresses.

"My heart bleeds for you," he snaps. "It must be a load on you, I'm sorry you're going through all this." He glares at me coldly and, before I know it, he is gone. I could punch myself in the face. He's right, I am being selfish. I get out of bed and rush to find him. I search the whole castle and do not locate him. He must have left but surely he will not attempt to get away for risk of killing again. I dash outside and run to the boat.

"Don't worry, it's still there." I hear his voice behind me.

"Sean, I've been so self-centered and I'm so sorry," I say as I turn to see his shadow in the moonlight. He says nothing and walks away.

"Sean," I call after him.

"Leave me alone. I need some space, Dest. I'll be back when I'm ready," he shouts over his shoulder. I have no option but to return. What have I done, I've been so stupid. I have spoiled our wonderful evening together and now I may have lost him, just when I had found him, and it's all my own stupid fault. I need to get the stick out of my derriere and lighten up a bit. I'm becoming tedious, this whole thing is changing me too. I should focus on setting myself right before I go looking to anyone else.

The hours tick by and he returns just minutes short of the time he is due to enter the dungeon and be safely ensconced for the day. I stand and wait for him to speak. I make no effort to approach him. He walks towards me and looks me right in the eye.

"You win, tomorrow we will search for answers," he says with a look of determination I have seen so many times before. I sigh with relief and, suddenly, he moves closer. I wonder what he intends to do, and then he puts his arm around my neck in a best buddy sort of way. "I'm tired, Dest. If we come up with nothing tomorrow, then please let it go. I think we know this is impossible but I am willing to try if it means this much to you."

"It does, Sean, and I promise, one night of planning and then we will put it aside forever."

"I want what little time I have left to be happy before I suffer who knows what for all eternity. I might as well be in hell as suffer what's coming."

"You're my soulmate, Sean. I will not allow it to happen."

"You said you'd do anything for me. Well, when I die, I want you to leave this place and never come back."

"It's time to go down, Sean." He looks me up and down before smirking. I raise my eyebrows and chuckle. "It's time, Sean."

"Promise me, Dest," he insists. I hesitate and then break a promise to myself, in order to make a promise to him.

"I will never look back," I reply.

"Thank you, Destiel." He kisses me on the cheek and then we head downstairs. It is *that* time once more.

Chapter 7

I let him out the following evening and he is true to his word, we discuss many options but none seem to provide a viable method of ensnaring the beast whilst also freeing Sean. It's impossible. There is only one way, and that is to get the Sior-Mabuz to take another host. I explain that I have racked my brains but it is all I can come up with. Sean will not hear of it.

"Please Sean," I beg. "If we can somehow get it to take on another, it will leave your body."

"I'm not doing it, Dest. I will not force anyone to trade places for *this*. Besides, it didn't leave the first guy, did it?"

"This is different. You are not fused as he was. It used that man to add flesh to itself, in order to survive and then he used him to become sentient and evolve as a human machine hybrid. As a result it is unable to fuse with your DNA and this is why your appearance still remains pure. When he is sleeping he disappears, which means you are not linked together as he is with the first man. It can only be *one* entity and it exists in combination with this man now. It is a whole person, just as you or I am."

"You don't know that for sure, Dest."

"I do. He does not need you. He is just using you to enable himself to fulfil his desires. This is what it does."

"How has this thing taken me then? I thought it was inside me."

"No, the nature of its attachment to you is more of a hold. It is simply keeping you hostage. The best way I can describe it is that it projects your form for its own advantage. It appears monstrous as itself. It knows it cannot pass for human and it wants to. Something happened when it became one with the human. The man's raw animal desires became twisted and corrupted and this is why it seems so evil. We need it to send its tendrils into someone else and it will move on from you. Just as you step from one tile to another on a pavement – your left foot reaches the next slab and your right foot leaves the one it is on. Well, this is how it is for machine tendrils."

"They made these things to do this to us? They use us to become superior versions of ourselves?" He sighs, "Once these bastards start coming through, there's no way we can beat them."

"No, Sean. They made these machines with the ability to replenish themselves through mechanical mutation. They do not know this has happened with organic matter. You're right, if they held this information they would most certainly use it against you, and the war against the robots would be over forever, there would be no more re-emergence. The ongoing cycle of war and peace would end. The human species would be permanently destroyed by machine infusion."

"Well, I don't wanna be around when they find out. Oh wait, hold on a minute, too late, I already am."

"They know nothing of this. True, it might only be a matter of time but that doesn't mean we can't save you."

"Destiel, you're talking about freakin' transhumanism… I never thought they would…"

"Sean, they have never found the key to this. They have tried many, many times but they have never found what makes transhumanism stick and work."

"Well, this dude sure knows," he says tapping his chest. He narrows his eyes, "It'll all be over, won't it?" I nod, I understand what he means. When this vital key component is discovered, humanity will be enslaved inside machines for all eternity. Almost like a complete recreation of the afterlife, when all living things become one with the source. No one will ever ascend and no one will ever procreate again. It will truly be the end of the human race.

"We have a chance," I reply. He knows I am evading the subject but does nothing to push the matter.

"I don't know, Dest. What if it just kills the person instead of entering them and hopping hosts? It won't work."

"Sean, this is not the first time this has been tried. There have been two other occasions when such a method was used after the creature had taken a hostage. We were able to get to them before it consumed them completely and altered their appearance forever."

"What? Why didn't you tell me this?" he says angrily. He has a right to feel this way. I should have told him. "What happened?" he asks urgently.

"On one occasion, the Sior-Mabuz used a woman in an effort to escape. When we attempted to withdraw the creature from her, so we could to kill it, she became weak and died. Although, we did manage to get her out first by getting the creature into a mouse. Sean, she *was* emancipated and she *did* die a free woman."

"But she did die, Destiel."

"You are not *her*, Sean."

"Destiel," he shouts as he stands up and begins pacing. "Why the hell would you keep this information secret?" He glares at me. I'm so ashamed but I truly believed this was not a viable option before.

"I thought it would darken your mood to know she had died. I'm sorry, Sean. I was thinking of you. Look, I didn't think it was anything we could use and I wanted to cause you as little pain as possible."

"Okay, so what happened to the mouse?" he asks. He has already taken this news on board, aligned his mind to the revelation and is readjusting his position. This is what makes him such a formidable opponent. He is always twenty steps ahead of everyone else.

"It was burnt up by the energy of the thing."

"Why did it take on the mouse? Surely it was too small."

"We managed to confuse it. The human part of it is very susceptible to drugs. We basically manipulated it. If it panics and believes it is in danger, it will morph into the nearest available living thing that moves, which is what it did. This is what the machines do, you've seen them mutate. Well, this is the same, except it uses organic material instead. It attempts to flee danger as any human would be compelled to do by their very nature. Well, the machine part of the Sior-Mabuz accommodates this desire to escape by using the method that has been encoded into it."

"Right!" He rubs his hand down his face. He is exasperated by this. "Destiel, you said there were two. Who else?"

"There was a man also. The Sior-Mabuz was far more prolific in his killing when this happened. He was able to kill many women by luring them to him through sympathy. It was back in 1948, and the man it took was very handsome, but war-injured…"

"Go on…" he says shaking his hand frantically. I stand up and get myself a glass of water, I am beginning to feel very uneasy. I regret this conversation but I know he will not leave this alone now. I gulp for way longer than is needed to quench my thirst, then I compose myself before continuing.

"It was again intoxicated, by getting the host subject to take a cocktail of drugs which saturated his cells, steadily inebriating the creature. Again, the Sior-Mabuz panicked when it felt threatened and his tendrils passed into the nearby dog we had placed in its path."

"How was the dog?" he asks, already half knowing the answer.

"He ran at first but… yes, he was burned up and subsequently died. My friend, someone I used to travel with, also died when the Sior-Mabuz used the dog's energy to get a stronghold on him."

"Why did you do it again when it had failed before?"

"It was believed that the larger animal would contain the Sior-Mabuz. Instead, it boosted its power to the point that it was able to kill. Fortunately, the mouse had very little to expend or we could have lost more the first time. It is regretful but we had to try."

"And the man it jumped out of, how was he?" he asks urgently as he brushes aside all questions as to why. He knows only too well that he would have done the same.

"He took a few breaths but died soon after from the trauma."

"And you want to do this to *me*?"

"Yes."

"Why would it be any different for me?" he asks. I sigh heavily. I do not have a definitive answer for this and it doesn't seem the right time to tell him it's because I believe he's different or special in some way.

"I am convinced it needs a *human* host replacement. If the transition is easier on the Sior-Mabuz, it will be less of a drain on the human it is releasing. It cannot digest the energy of a different species as effectively. It is now part human after all."

"Because of the first man? I guess this makes sense," he says. Sean is no fool in these matters.

"Also, you are not the average person. You are so much stronger and tougher. I know you will make it." I smile and he shakes his head in refusal. "It's a solution, Sean." I frown anxiously, and I sense he is considering the option carefully.

"I agree, Dest, it is a way out. Risky but I would rather die than stay this way."

We gaze at each other for a few moments. He is thinking it through. We both know the creature cannot be killed and, even if it could, we both know Sean would be killed along with it, but it seems Sean is willing to sacrifice his life for his soul's freedom. The scenario of our passing over the host subject is ideal for this. If Sean lives through the ordeal – a great outcome, but if he dies, at least his soul is free.

"It's the best option, Sean. Whether you live or die, it's for the best. Your soul is worth taking the risk for." I emphasis my position in the hope of prompting him to agree. "You won't die, I just know it. You're too strong. The war has lifted your level of endurance to the max. You will get through it." I desperately want him back the way he was and I am willing to try anything, and say anything, to keep him with me. I have no idea whether the human transition thing would work, I'm sure it would but I can't be certain. I just need to convince him it will. I have no real way of knowing if he would survive but I have faith in him.

"I won't do it, no," he says sharply. "If I force this destiny on another man, my soul will go to hell anyway - same difference." We both sigh and I know there is nothing else that can be done. "Are you sure we can't just politely ask it to get the hell out of me?" he says with a weak smile.

"Well, we could try. He is a reasonable guy after all," I reply. We laugh and I beckon Sean to me. "Come here," I say and he joins me on the couch. I know he is worried. It has been a trying evening and I realize we are no further on than we were before. I do my best to lighten the mood.

It is soon almost time to return Sean to the basement.

"Sean, we need to go down soon," I whisper, breaking the silence which has come between us for the past hour.

"I know, I know," he says softly. "Destiel, promise me something? No more lies huh?" He has been thinking about this, he is wondering whether he can trust me. I have let him down badly.

"I was trying to protect you. It's because I love you so much. But I promise, truth. Cross my heart." He turns to me and smiles briefly. I think there is a part of him that understands why I did what I did. He has made similar decisions in the past. He knows that it is often necessary to hold back.

"Dest, tell me. How do you know that my soul will be imprisoned? Surely, if I die then it will leave my body."

"No, it has no escape. It is essentially a tessellation, a tapestry of energy, and this energy cannot be impeded when it ascends. If it is hampered in any way at all, then the fragile carrier, the soul's transport to the afterlife, will disintegrate causing the soul to be trapped."

"Well, how do you know that? I mean, do we even have a soul? Sometimes I wonder."

"Yes, of course. I know this for sure. I have seen many."

"How?" he says as he promptly sits up and faces me. It's obvious he is shocked. We are forbidden from telling inhabitants of the past about the future. We are ordered to interact with people as little as possible when we journey through time but I see no harm in telling him now. It doesn't matter to me anymore. It's not like I can ever return and I already know the future will continue to change as these things evolve. One person knowing something before their time will make little difference to the outcome.

"We have ascension ceremonies. Like you have funerals. The undertaker casts the rapture rays upon the body, and then we watch as the essence of that person leaves. We witness the God take the soul."

"Sounds creepy, you sure it's not a hologram?"

"I'm sure. It's a very beautiful and comforting sight. Although, I must say, it has crossed my mind it may merely be a trick. Nevertheless, it is effective and keeps

God to the forefront of the human mind. It keeps people in line."

"Keeps you in line?" he gasps with a horrified frown. "Why does such a beloved God need to keep anyone in line?"

"There are two options. You rise to him and dwell eternally in paradise… or you descend. The second option is limited in its appeal. Nobody wants to go there and so everyone obeys."

"Do the bad guys get a ceremony?" he asks with a sceptical glare.

"In a manner of speaking. The Chasm is broadcast at a specified time each day and all the nations of the world are compelled to watch on pain of death. If we are not observed watching the ritual then we join the condemned souls the following day. I can't even begin to describe the terror. If you were to see The Chasm then, believe me, you too would do everything in your power to resist going there."

"Sounds like this God of yours is kinda manipulative and controlling, Dest."

"Well, he's not my God anymore. He does not approve of me loving you and so I do not approve of him. I am gradually moving away from this so-called religion."

"What's my soul matter then?" he laughs.

I pull him to me and kiss him, "Because there might just be a better God."

We leave for the basement and, once the Sior-Mabuz has taken over, I stand in front of it. It hisses at me and attempts to get to me.

"It's me, Sean," I say, and I sense it mellow. It looks me in the eye.

"Please may I have my friend back?" I ask it. Its head tilts to one side and I feel it might have understood me, and then it makes a sinister face. It would seem the thing is laughing at me. I realize I will not get anywhere bargaining with it. I know then that all hope is lost. I return upstairs and weep. I know I have to let it go, Sean is lost to me.

I have to distract myself and so I decide to take a walk around the grounds. The weather has picked up a little today and the gardens are very beautiful. I wish Sean could share this moment with me but I know he may never again see natural light, and *I* may never again see the sunshine glint in his eyes. I wonder how much longer we will have together. I have noticed that Sean's appearance has changed slightly, he looks thinner and weaker somehow. I put the thought far from my mind as I take in fresh air in the hope of pulling some optimism in through my lungs.

I get around to the other side of the castle and suddenly, I know that I am not alone. I read a person's mind. This is the first time I have done such a thing for quite some time and it takes me by surprise. This person's intention is to hide before they are seen by me. I pretend I am unaware and continue on my way. I soon realize it is Connell and wonder why he has hidden himself from my view. I trace his footsteps in my mind. I mentally note his whereabouts so I can find out where he has gone. I take out my knife, just in case, and hide behind a garden wall, allowing him to believe I have returned to the house.

Perhaps he is checking up on me and then my mind plays out a terrible scene and I am unsure of what I am seeing. There is so much violence involved. I decide that I will take a look around later and see what I find. Perhaps I can also attempt to read his thoughts when he has gone home. I have done it over great distances before. I decide I must tell Sean about this incident. I would not have done so before now, in order to keep him from worry, but I have promised to be honest and I intend to keep my promise to him. I secretly watch as Connell takes his boat and leaves. I believe Sean's instincts about this man's intentions might have been spot on.

I make up my mind to check the place where I had envisioned him being. I have nothing else to do and perhaps it will turn out to be something interesting that I can tell Sean about later. He could do with some kind of distraction. I come across an old wartime shelter. It is hidden beneath the grass. I wonder what he has in there that he needs to keep secret. The door is only pulled closed and so I enter, careful not to disturb anything. I find it's just an old tool shed. I suppose he uses it for storage and he needed something from it. I make the assumption he avoided me in an attempt to escape the food shopping again. It could have even been because he was afraid I would ask him to enter the dungeon for some reason. It would not surprise me if this was the case. Knowing this thing dwells there is one thing, but coming face to face with it is quite another.

I turn around and am about to leave, when I notice a bloodied shirt squeezed behind the table. I do not touch it but move as close as the table top will allow. I take a look and realize it belongs to a woman. I begin to worry. Within moments, my mind plays out all sorts of scenarios. My brain is working overtime. This whole experience is making me jumpy. I move towards the logical conclusion that he probably cut himself and the woman's blouse is most likely one his partner has given him to use as a rag. I chuckle to myself. This situation is starting to get to me, talk about paranoia. I take a slow walk back, keen to pass the time until evening comes. I later remotely read Connells mind. It turns up nothing. It would seem his focus is on getting to the pub as quickly as possible. Connell has done nothing wrong. His sole existence is one of sloth. We have nothing to fear from him. In fact, his tendency towards the more iniquitous side of life is a useful ally to us. It keeps him fully occupied, there is no room for anything else.

Chapter 8

I am pleased to see Sean at dinner, and I let him know all about what I have seen. I tell him how worried I was until I tracked Connell's mind as he prepared for an evening out at the bar and realised he was more concerned with getting drunk. We laugh and it takes our minds away from what we are going through. It feels good to let these things go for a while and I sense a strong spark between us. This is how things would be if we could be together properly. I imagine us living together and a knot of anticipation creeps into my stomach. I can't keep myself from looking at him. It seems so long since I touched him. There's a part of me that wants to rip his clothes off and another part that just wants to hold him tight forever. This is all so new to me. I have not led a simple life and others have often been in awe of the things I have gotten to do. It might seem exciting and it is, but there is no feeling in the world that can match the elation I feel when Sean and I are together. He throws me some smouldering glances and I know he wants me too. When we are finished, he stands and holds out his hand. I take it and he leads me to the bedroom. I am almost dizzy as we walk, my heart is pounding so hard. I know he must feel the same. This is like a dream come true to me, it's all I have yearned for since I met him.

We are desperate to get to each other and I begin to undress quickly. Sean follows my lead and we rush to each other's arms. Our bodies meet and then our lips. Sean puts his hand behind my head and my whole body tingles from his touch.

I open my eyes as he slides his lips from mine and smiles. He then playfully pushes me onto the bed and I fall back. His face is flushed and I can see in his eyes just how much he wants me. I want him too and I laugh nervously as he lowers himself down until he is hovering just above me. He runs his hand through my hair, pushing it back and, before I know it, I can feel his heart pounding against mine as his full weight is upon me. I am smothered by him and I enjoy the feeling of being helpless as I give in to my desire to give myself to him completely. I moan as he kisses my neck and I slide my arms around his warm body and trace my finger along his back. He quivers as I do so, and I hear him whisper my name before he moves me onto my side and brings himself in close to me. I can feel him pressed tightly up to me.

"Sean," I gasp as I breathe deeply and inhale the love between us. He slides his arm around me and strokes my body as I turn to him and open my mouth so he can get his tongue in there.

His kiss tastes sweet and when he touches me, I feel like I am in paradise. I rub my hand along his thigh as I moan in pleasure as a stirring feeling swirls in my chest. I need to get closer to him and so I turn around to face him. I want to look into his sparkling eyes.

"I've never loved anyone like this," he says and I swallow hard. I never imagined I would ever hear those words from him. "You're all I ever want," he says as he moves his hand gently over my back.

"You have to mean that, Sean," I say and he smiles as he puts his mouth to mine and I feel it. I feel the love pass from him to me and I know that he is mine and, as we make love, I know that we will never be torn apart no matter what. We will find a way to be together forever.

I am happy and drowsy as we lay together afterwards, and I allow my eyes to close, only for them to be forced open again when I hear a noise that startles me. I listen intently, and there it is again. It is someone sneaking around outside the door. I'm sure of it.

"Sean," I say quietly. "There's someone here… listen."

"I don't hear anything," he says sleepily as he pulls me in close to him.

"It's probably just my imagination," I reply as I lay uneasily back down. Then, before we are aware of what is happening, the door has opened and we hear a booming voice.

"What's going on here then?" We look up to see Connell stood in the doorway. I can't believe this. This is something we could do without. I mean, what the hell is he doing here in the middle of the night?

"I can explain," I say quickly. I have to say something but I can see he is not pleased at all we are here.

"The dungeon is empty. You two been taking the piss outta me," he snaps. "There *isn't* a Sior-Mabuz." His eyes bore into us. I think if I had been alone it would have been okay, he wouldn't even have minded that the creature was missing.

"It's inside me," Sean blurts as he sits up and looks directly at Connell.

"The only thing inside you, boy, is him," he says pointing at *me*.

"Oh get over yourself," Sean says dismissively.

"I thought you was a bit too human looking," Connell snarls.

"Shame I can't say the same about you," Sean retaliates. I know I must smooth the situation over and I attempt to explain that the creature only awakens during the day. He appears to believe this to a certain extent but he doesn't seem to care. He will not tolerate us being here. To him, accommodating our relationship is worse than housing the Sior-Mabuz.

"Whatever, I'm not having your sort round here sponging off my hospitality. You make me sick, the two of you. On your bike," he says indicating to the door with his thumb.

"*Really?*" Sean says. "You call this hospitable?"

"I said, on your bike asshole."

"You throw us out and I'll make sure that the Sior-Mabuz calls on you first." Sean smiles and the man shakes his head in disbelief. "You wanna chance it?" Sean adds to back up his position.

We watch as Connell paces the room. It's clear he doesn't want to take the chance. I hear his mental dialogue and am aware he is trying to reach a compromise. He wants us gone, that's for sure but he's scared.

"Two more nights and then you're out, the two of you."

"Yes, of course," I agree. This will at least buy us time. The man stands glaring at us.

"You not got a wife to get home to," Sean says. "Or you gonna stand there all night."

"I got no one to rush home to. Don't you worry about me."

"Okay then, I won't," Sean replies with a shrug.

"I'll be back, night after next. You better not be here or I'll hit you so hard his future self will feel it," he says to Sean as he points towards me. Then he slams the door shut behind him.

We get up and head out of the room. I glance out of the window and see him walk away. I breathe a sigh of relief that he is no longer hanging about.

"We'll have to kill him," Sean says as he stands behind me and puts his arms around my waist.

"We can't," I say with a chuckle. "It's not a bad idea though."

"You heard him, no one will miss him," Sean says and I remember the ripped blouse in the shed.

"There's someone… he has female clothing in his shelter."

"Maybe it's his," Sean says. "Live and let live, Dest."

"Sean, this isn't funny." I say as I smile to myself.

"Hey, I'm serious," he says.

"I know you are," I reply, raising my eyebrows.

"This place is pretty nice for an abandoned hideout, don't you think?" Sean says as he walks away and gestures around.

"Maybe he has someone come here and he aims to impress," I say attempting to find a reason for the luxurious abode. It had never been kept to anywhere near a high a standard in the past. Especially when his grandfather maintained it. He was terrified to come here. He made sure the outside looked okay and that was it. He never even came inside. This guy is different though, he's definitely not afraid to enter the place, especially if he has been to the dungeon. I can't help but wonder if he has been there before. Perhaps I was wrong and he has seen the creature. "It is possible he brings a girlfriend here."

"Are you kidding, did you see the state of him?" Sean laughs. "He's repulsive."

I glance back to the window and there is no sign of him. I am worried, for Sean. What will become of him if I leave him here imprisoned, alone with that man free to enter that dungeon anytime he likes. With Sean chained up, he will be totally at his mercy. It's clear that this is something we are going to have to face. We will just have to hope that Connell stays out of that dungeon and does not harm Sean.

"I shall call him tomorrow, smooth things over. I'll make some sort of bargain with him so you can stay while I leave immediately. This will pacify him."

"Like hell you will, you promised me, Dest."

"Things have changed," I say sternly.

"That's it, I'm going to find him and kill him with my bare hands and if I don't get there in time to do it, the Sior-Mabuz will."

"This is anger talking, Sean."

"Damn it. I'm in love with you, Destiel," he shouts. I turn to see him in tears. "Don't leave me by myself," he says, and my heart melts to see him this way. "You promised me," he cries.

"Okay, okay," I say as I hold him and he buries his head in my arms and sobs. "Please don't be upset. We'll figure something out. Look, let's get out of here for a while," I suggest calmly. I now know that Sean is not strong enough to withstand this alone.

"Let's go to that hideout of his, dig some dirt on him. We might find something to use against him, Dest."

"I like this idea," I smile.

We make our way outside and I find my way back to the old shelter. I start to follow the direction of my torch and then a light goes on. I swiftly turn to see Sean smiling as he holds the light pull string. I laugh and we begin to search. I am long past caring whether we disturb anything. We find nothing but old tools and then I get a snatch of an image. It is so vivid it hurts my head.

"What is it, Dest," Sean asks as he runs to me and holds me up.

"I don't know, something strange. I feel there is evil here, Sean, and before you say it, I don't mean the creature."

"How do you mean then?" he asks staring at me. "Do you sense that Connell guy has been up to no good?"

"Yes. I believe so."

"He's hurt someone hasn't he? You can see it in a man's eyes. I've seen it enough. You want to have seen them on the field, Dest. It was way back before I moved onto being an agent. It was just one of the minor scuffles but it was still hell on earth. There's the ones who are there firing their weapon in the hopes of killing a human instead of a robot. They want to see the life drain from a person's eyes. It comes natural to them to hurt people. The wars are just an excuse."

"I'm sorry you've had to experience that, Sean."

"This whole war is down to men like him. There's nothing inside them. Gotta fill their lives with something."

"They don't change in time," I say sadly. Gradually he is revealing more about his life to me. The stuff that he has locked away for so long, things he himself has almost forgotten exists. I take him out of that place and we sit by the river for a time and he tells me about what he endured when fighting over the years. I have new respect for him with every word and my awareness of my own part in it all becomes clearer. I feel that I may have added to his turmoil by popping up in his life and asking for assistance whenever times got rough. It never occurred to me that he just wanted to be left alone for a while to get on with living. I have not had an easy life but have I escaped much of the pain of the wars, which I am grateful for. Sometimes machines are good, if it wasn't for ours in the future, we would most certainly be slaves.

"Look, what are we going to do?" he asks, breaking the unspoken promise we made to sit and ignore it. I shrug my shoulders.

"I don't know," I reply, "but I do know Connell is a nasty piece of work. He's trouble, that's for sure. I will tell him I know he has hurt someone. I just hope the potential exposure of his crime forces him to let us alone."

"Well, I don't know if it'll work but give it your best shot, Dest. If anyone can talk him round, you can," he says as he stands up and brushes himself down.

"Sean, if we ever get out of this what's going to happen?"

"Between us?" he asks as he skims a stone across the water. "Reckon that was seven there, Dest."

I smile as I pick up a stone and move towards him. "Move aside," I say as I toss it across the Loch.

Chapter 9

"You can't prove anything," Connell says. "So I get a little carried away sometimes. Best of luck proving that one." He laughs and hangs up on me. I realize this tactic won't work, he knows he has us over a barrel. I vow that I will kill him myself if he does anything to harm Sean. I know he has murdered someone, maybe more than one. How I never spotted his true nature, I don't know. I had the impression he was an okay guy before, how wrong can a person be? I tell Sean as soon as I see him and he grunts in acknowledgement. He appears so weak and there are clear signs of decay, he looks bruised and there is a hefty cut above his eye. I imagine it happened during the day when he was unaware. Nevertheless, it must be painful to wake up to these injuries every night. This thing does not have enough energy to keep replenished. Eventually, Sean's image will fade and he will appear as the Sior-Mabuz even when the creature is asleep. I cannot bear this to happen. I get him upstairs and tend to his wounds and look after him. He is so precious to me and *I* hurt to see *him* hurt.

We attempt to carry on as normal and forget it all for a while but this is not to be. We quietly share a meal together but are interrupted when we hear a sound on the stairs. We both look to the door and see Connell walk arrogantly inside.

"Still here, eh ladies?" he says before turning around again. "I'll be back tomorrow. You'd better not be here."

"Get back here," I call after him as he exits the doorway. "You know we can't just leave."

"Yes you can," he replies. "I took a look in that dungeon today and saw that thing in there, and now it's out." He points at Sean and then at me, "and you let it out."

"And your point is?" Sean asks.

"I dunno what you are, but I don't want you here any longer. On your bike, I mean it, okay," he shouts.

"Or what?" I ask.

"I'll kill the pair of you, and plant you in the back garden. You see if I don't."

"Good luck, Pal, I'm immortal," Sean smiles. We watch Connell fumble as he realizes it's true. "So what you gonna do?"

"Hey, it didn't stick around before," he laughs holding up his arms. "Aye, that's right, it was me that let it out. Here's fifty pence, away and phone the judge."

Sean dives to his feet and begins belting the man over and over until he falls to the floor. He persists when he is down and I make a grab for him but he shrugs me off and continues the abuse. He is letting everything out and taking it out on Connell's face. I get to him again and drag him away by the arm. I hold him back as he struggles to get to the man to issue more punishment. I manage to stop him before he does some serious damage but as my back is turned, Connell clobbers me with something heavy and I fall to the ground. The next thing I know is that Sean has taken matters into his own hands. I watch through blurred vision as he attacks Connell with everything he has. I call out to him as I lose consciousness and everything fades to black.

I awake, hazy-eyed, on the couch sometime later. I am unsure how long I have been asleep but I feel like I have been out of it for hours. I feel terrible. I scan the room and see Sean lying on the other seat. His head is rested on a pillow and he is far away in thought. I wonder if he has killed the man.

"Sean," I croak, and he rushes to me.

"Hey, you took quite a blow there, Dest. Are you okay?" he asks as he puts his arm around me.

"I'm fine, just a bit of a headache. Are *you* okay?" I say as I stroke my hand across his face. He grabs it and kisses it before holding it to him.

"Don't worry about me, I can take care of myself."

"And Connell? Is he dead?" I ask fearing the answer. I take a swift look at the clock. We have less than two hours before sun up.

"He's fine. You know, Destiel, I've changed my mind, I…"

"Hey, I said I'm not leaving you…"

"No, I don't mean that," he says and then he pauses and bites his bottom lip. It's something he does when he's about to say something controversial. I've seen him do it so many times before that it's enough to make me anxious about what's coming next.

"What is it," I say as I sit up. "You have me worried."

"This Connell dude is not a nice guy. He let that thing escape, it's because of him all those people are dead." He thrusts his finger into his chest, "And he's the reason I'm trapped in here."

"Sean, what's your point?" I ask wanting him to get to the gist of it. "What have you done?" I feel I am going to explode with worry.

"Okay, we'll do it. We'll try your plan. We'll transfer the Sior-Mabuz into *him*."

"Really? You sure you want to?" I say. I can't believe he is prepared to do it but he is right. This man deserves it for having unleashed the beast. If someone has to pay the price, why not the one who did it?

"Those people in Glasgow deserve justice. That woman's he's killed and buried here somewhere. Well, what about her? Doesn't her life mean anything?"

"Of course, Sean, but it's not your responsibility…"

"He hurt you too, Dest. I won't let him hurt you again."

"You need to it for yourself, Sean. Not to stop me, or anyone else, getting hurt."

"I will," he says softly. "Dest, you must've noticed my bruises and my…"

"Memory lapses?" I say as I rub his arm to comfort him.

"I feel like I'm half asleep. You know, in *here*," he says as he smacks his forehead. "I'm dying and I don't mean just mean physically, but mentally too. I'm losing it."

"I know." I reply. "Sean, I wish you would share these things with me. I want to go through it with you, be there for you."

"You are there for me, Dest. I couldn't have got through his whole crazy thing if you weren't here. Will you help me do it?"

"You know I will. When I said I'd do anything for you, I meant it. You're my world."

"If you want to you can walk away now. You don't have to do it," he says raising his hands emphatically.

"I want to. I want to spend the rest of my life with you," I reply before grabbing him and kissing him deeply. I can't believe it, I'm going to get him back... just the way he was.

Sean tells me he has Connell imprisoned in the cellar and so we head down there to check he is secure. I hope he doesn't kick off again. I don't think either of us has the strength to fight him. When we arrive he is different.

"Look, Destiel, I'm sorry about the head. You can understand can you not? It was a shock. Look, I use this place all the time. Why is that a problem, I do own it. If you chain him up, lock the door and go on your way, we'll say no more about it, what do you say?" He shrugs his shoulders and I see Sean wince as his chains rattle. "Well?" Sean and I look at each other. "Come on, give us peace, let me out. Please? I'm not staying here with that thing. What if it escapes and eats me?"

"I tell you what, we'll think about it," I say and then I lock Sean down opposite him, leaving enough gap that the Sior-Mabuz cannot reach him. I then kiss Sean as Connell makes snide remarks. I ignore him and make for the stairs. He picks up the level of abuse as he notices me leaving and begins to screech at me as I walk out the door. I can't help but snigger, it will do him good to have a little rendezvous with the Sior-Mabuz. Let them get acquainted, they *are* going to spend eternity together after all.

When I return that evening, I see that Connell is asleep. I untie Sean and see that he appears to be very weak. I help him to find his footing before sliding his arm around my shoulder so I can take his weight.

"If we are to do this, Dest, it needs to be soon," he says.

"Come on, let's get you out of here," I say as he falls into me. We creep past Connell and lock the dungeon door behind us.

"That guy screamed all day, I could hear it somewhere deep inside but I couldn't stop that animal flinging itself towards him. He's done in. That was cruel, Dest."

"So you're aware then?" I ask. "I thought this might be so."

"On some level, I am, yeah. I get awoken and become more alert, the more it pulls and screams."

"Hey, you're not going soft on Connell are you? Sean, we have to do this."

"Don't worry, I'm still up for it."

When we get upstairs, I take him into the bathroom, where he takes off his clothes and I inspect his body. He's still beautiful but he's covered in cuts and bruises, which I carefully clean and dress. The old injuries are no longer healing but I do what I can to make them appear better so he doesn't notice. I know it must be painful for him but he is too stubborn to complain. He is swaying slightly and so I throw the cloth down into the sink and help him to sit on the edge of the bath. He takes a hold of me as I do so and pulls me towards him.

"Thank you, Destiel," he says before tenderly kissing me.

"Come on, let's get you tucked up in bed," I say as I escort him from the bathroom. He stumbles along the way and then steadies himself on the bedpost "You lay yourself down and I'll bring you something to eat and drink."

"Is there much food left," he asks.

"Yes, enough for a few more days," I say but he has eaten so much that I need to lie a little. Well, there is sort of enough, it's a half-truth. There is enough for one and I know he needs it more. When I return, I see he has fallen asleep. I get into bed next to him and snuggle for a while, I just want to be close to him for a few moments. If our plans don't work out as they should, I might lose him very soon

I kiss him gently, whisper that I love him and then leave him to rest for a couple of hours He looked exhausted this evening and we have to work quickly. We need him strong enough for what we must do. I think through ways of getting the transfer to work and eventually come up with something that might just do it. I hunt high and low through the castle for things which might be of assistance to us. I regret leaving him alone in case he needs me but it is necessary if we are going to make this work. There are so many rooms in this castle and it is difficult to know which junk might come in handy but I am surprised to find stuff which can be adapted for our needs. Fortunately, there is whiskey in the cellar next to the dungeon, no doubt Connell's secret stash. This can be used for purposes of intoxication. I also see there are strong painkillers in a bathroom cabinet in one of the other rooms. They are past their expiration but they will help Sean to feel better. They might also enhance the intoxication of the drink. Whiskey alone should do the trick but Sean is no stranger to a drink and so, if it is potentiated by the painkillers, the extra boost will give us a failsafe. Combined, the cocktail might just work and be powerful enough to inebriate Sean, which will, in turn, subdue the beast.

"Dest," I hear him call out to me as I return to the room and I rush to his bedside.

"What is it, Sean," I say and he smiles.

"I just wanted to make sure you were still here," he says grabbing me. He is trembling with fear and I suspect he has had a nightmare. It's not surprising given the circumstances.

"I wouldn't abandon you in this condition, Sean." I can't believe he would think I might. "I just briefly stepped out to find equipment. I didn't want to wake you. Your strength will be needed to get you through. Here, take some of these they should help." I pass him two of the pills. He leans forward and swallows them with a large gulp of water and then flops back down.

I sit with him for a while and he looks slightly better after a few hugs and kisses, and so I reheat his dinner and fetch it to him. Slowly, he manages to eat. I can tell he's forcing himself. I sit opposite him and watch him chew every mouthful and then urge him to drink the tropical fruit juice I have brought him.

"I hate that stuff," he groans.

"You need the vitamins… please? For me?" I plead. He grabs the glass and drinks it in one before wiping his hand across his mouth.

"Yum," he says with a grin.

"Thank you for humouring me, Sean."

"Dest, come and lie with me for a while?" he says as he pats the bed. I agree and lie down by his side. The bed is warm and soft and I struggle to keep my eyes open. I just want this over.

"You know, my family and friends would have a fit if they knew what was happening between you and me." He closes his eyes and I wonder where those words came from. Perhaps he is considering the consequences of our being together in the real world. I guess that's good, he is looking to the future and is in hope of getting out of here. Still, there seems to be a worry about how the relationship will be perceived. I have never heard him talk about anyone close to him before and so I sense this is important, but I make no attempt to get any more out of him. I figure he will tell me when he is ready. I tell him my plan.

"I think it might work but I don't know if I'm strong enough to do it tonight."

"Is that because it's easier to be with me while we are trapped in this place?"

"How do you mean?"

"You're anticipating what will happen once we leave? You do want to be together when we leave don't you?" I ask concerned I might be losing him already.

"Yes, I do. I'm not going to drop you once I get free. You worry too much. I just want one more day to recover is all."

"You might be weaker still tomorrow," I suggest, hoping to urge him to action.

"It's a chance I'll have to take. My legs feel like lead. Its energy zapping fending that thing off all night. Maybe we could put that guy, Connell, somewhere else. He's driving that freak crazy and I'm feeling the brunt of it. The angrier it gets, the more I get flung about."

"Yes, okay, but I think hiding him in there behind something might be better, at least then he won't escape. We need him and we need him alive, Sean."

"Dest, I do love you, you know," he says out of the blue.

"What would they say if they knew I was your guy?" I ask as I look for signs of worry on his face and attempt to read his mind, which I cannot.

"My parents would probably have a heart attack. My mother wants me to settle down now I'm nearing thirty but I don't think you're what she had in mind. She would be cool with it after a while though," he smiles. I feel relieved when he says this. "It's the rest of them, they wouldn't get it, especially the guys. They wouldn't understand and they would think I'd been living a lie all these years. They'll tell me they don't like this sort of thing, and I'm sure I will hear this repeatedly, and that's if they still talk to me at all. You'd understand this, what with that strict God of yours."

"Tell me something about your life, Sean. I know very little about you. You know, from before you joined the fight."

"You know everything about me. The war is all there is. I've been fighting these things since forever."

"No, I mean from before we ever met. Before you pledged to fight the robots and became an insider on the real nature of the conflict. There must be something."

"Been fighting since I was a kid," he says and I sigh. I should've guessed he'd never open up fully. He closes his eyes, then, to my surprise, he tells me everything.

I had no idea what he had been through. It seems Sean's early life wasn't happy. His parents separated when he was very young and he had a string of stepfathers, many of whom were unkind. He was so lonely, and I imagine this is why he never gets close to anyone. It has become a defence mechanism, an

120

ingrained habit. I feel privileged that he has opened up to me and trusts me enough to share parts of his life with me.

Chapter 10

Around an hour later, I begin to notice that Sean is looking much healthier. I think the painkillers are a blessing. Thank God I found them.

"Dest, what are we going to do if someone comes looking for Connell?" he asks as he starts to get dressed.

"He said he has nobody and even if he has, they haven't come yet. If we can get him chained up, any of his family looking for him will know of the legend. It's a close kept family secret but they have all been made aware of the existence of the Sior-Mabuz. They needed to be, for their own safety. If a person is chained in that spot, they will know the Sior-Mabuz has taken possession of him. If they come at night and he is himself, I'm sure they will be canny enough to wait it out until daylight to check his condition. This is what I would do."

"That's *you*, not everyone has your brains, Dest. You're used to this stuff." He pulls on his shoes and then looks at me. "I hope you're right."

"Are you up to it?" I ask, wanting to get this over with as quickly as possible.

"I'm not sure, Dest, what do you think?"

"It depends how you feel, Sean. I think you can do it. How strong are you right now?"

"I just don't know, it depends how we're going to do this, Dest. I mean, how will we make the transfer? I'm not sure I can fight that thing like this," he says as he throws his hands and they land with a slap on his legs.

We make our way to the living room and he walks up and down. He's uneasy about it. There's just so much that can go wrong.

"We need to get the Sior-Mabuz close enough to the man to get it to eject its tendrils and send them into his flesh. It will use him to escape if it feels threatened, I'm sure of that. This thing cannot see past its own nose when in fear, and it *will* use whatever is at hand to ensure the survival of the machine element of its make up."

"How do you know it has to feel threatened? Maybe it doesn't like the feeling of not being in control, and so tries to take back the power. I reckon it's on an ego trip that's got out of hand."

"This might be true to a certain extent, but it would not have taken on animal form unless it felt it had to. This would be like us wanting to become merged with something non-human, it's just not going to happen. The very fact it did… well… this is a clear sign it felt it needed to tendril and traffic."

"But this is a *human* we're talking about. If it sees Connell - a free human who is available, then it might just make the leap without us having to threaten it in any way."

"What if it doesn't," I say emphatically. "Connell is quite unattractive and this thing will not take on an ugly form."

"I reckon it would use his body until it can find someone else. It's just a stop gap for it while it finds something better to drive into. That's what I would do."

"This is true but if the other man is chained, then it will not have the freedom to leap. There is no way we are going to get Connell to sit next to the thing either, Sean."

"We could knock him out or get him drunk, but I guess it's the same situation, he's still trapped and *you* can't be in there, Dest, because it'll go for you. That means I'm alone with it and if it does manage to wake up in Connells body, then I lose my throat and he walks free. There's no way I can get out of there without it killing me. Look, Dest, I'm tired of this. I don't mind..."

"You don't mind what?" I say turning swiftly towards him. "No, I won't let you give up your life, Sean. I just won't."

"It might be the only way, Dest. I don't want to die but I want to be in that thing even less."

I stand up and pace the floor. I will not let this happen. We didn't come all this way for me to lose him now. There must be something, I just need to think of a way out of this.

"Maybe we should just leave the whole thing," Sean says as I return to my chair.

"Stop it, Sean. Just stop it. I'm not going to let you die. Forget it."

"Okay, okay, sorry I spoke," he says as he sniggers and rolls his eyes. Maybe the self-pity will stop now. I cannot stand this awful self-indulgence. I run my fingers through my hair. I feel like I may cry, my emotions are becoming so much harder to control.

"We need it running scared," I say. "This way it leaves you, moves away and you have a chance to escape. The question is, how can we make it want to get away *and* make Connell appear to be an unchained, ready to run human vessel?"

"How the hell will I outrun it when I'm drunk?" he asks impatiently. I ignore the attitude he has suddenly adopted. He is obviously pissed at me for putting him in place. At least he's stopped with the tragic self-sacrifice, I'd take the attitude above *that* anytime.

"We'll cross that bridge when we come to it. For now we need to concentrate on getting that thing to take Connell in a run for its life. This will not be easy."

"Easy? You talk about an eternity in the Mabuz but we're going to spend an eternity here trying to figure this shit out," Sean says shaking his head and smirking.

"Stop being so defeatist, Sean. Anyone would think you didn't want to escape."

"Are you kidding? Oh… just Shut up, Destiel." He sighs and pulls on his sweater over the top of his tee-shirt, "Come on, let's take a walk down to that cellar and collect the whiskey. The cold air will clear our heads." I nod in agreement. This seems like a good way to cool the atmosphere between us. "Is it near the dungeon?" he asks as he pulls open the door.

"Yes. It's inside the trap door but not so far down as the dungeon." He looks worried. "Don't worry." I say, following him as he leads the way, thankfully he has let his irritation slide. We traipse slowly down the staircase, neither of us willing to expend more energy than is necessary. He stops when he reaches the bottom. "Where is it again?" he asks. I point to the trapdoor and then smile sympathetically, realizing he is very aware of his lapses in memory. I hope this is something which would not continue should he find freedom from slavery. Who knows how far his memory will be damaged before we find an escape for him. I don't think I could bear it if Sean wasn't *Sean* anymore.

"The whiskey is down in the dungeon?" he shrieks with a look of horror. He has forgotten what I said as we left the room. This is getting worse than I thought.

"Yes, I told you it wa…" I stop myself, not wanting to point out further memory flaws. "It is, yes, but not quite as far down, just about half way. It's that wooden door on the mezzanine level."

"The what?" he asks and I take a deep breath before repeating myself. I'm a little exasperated at his lack of understanding. He can be quite ignorant at times.

"There is a door half way down the steps which leads to the dungeon. It's a huge, fat, oak door to the right? Remember?" I wonder how afraid of the dungeon he actually is. It must be all the more awful for him to face this added fear every day. I attempt to soothe him, "It's not right down in there where you get chained up." I watch as he takes a deep breath. "You don't have to go down if you don't want to, Sean."

"I want to," he says as he brushes past me and flings open the hatch with surprisingly little effort. We descend quietly and he manages locate the door on the right which leads to the cellar. "I just hope Connell doesn't hear us walking around." I look at him and notice he is shaking slightly. He appears to be more jumpy than he usually is when entering the lower staircase. I wonder what has happened to cause his anxiety level to soar, but I dare not ask for fear of making it worse. I have a nagging thought that it is the memory issues, it is almost like he is going through it for the first time all over again.

"Connell won't be able to hear anything," I assure him. "The walls and floors are too thick. The sounds won't pass through the stones. Just keep your voice down and we'll be fine." He nods and opens the door quietly as a few butterflies whip past us.

"I hate those things," he says as he swipes at his face.

"Brace yourself then, this cellar is full of them," I say as Sean enters the room. "There's a pull-on light somewhere around here," I whisper as I aim my torch and feel around, eventually pulling on the string which illuminates the cellar enough for me to see Sean busy flapping at the butterflies. "Sean, get a grip, it's just a few butterflies," I say.

"Well you wouldn't say that if you'd woken up to them buzzing around your head every night. They're trying to get their larvae under my skin. I just know it."

"How have they gotten down there into the dungeon," I ask before becoming distracted when I hear Connell shout.

"You two clowns better not be at my stash," he roars.

"I thought he couldn't hear us," Sean says as we both look around bemused. "You couldn't pass me down a bottle while you're there could you, boys? Help me pass away the time until I get outta here and kill the two of you." We hunt around to find out how we are able to hear his voice. Eventually, after managing to move aside a heavy cabinet, we see there are slat holes at the base of the cellar wall. It seems there are some vents which allow for the circulation of air from dungeon to cellar.

"This is how the butterflies have gotten through," I say quietly as Sean peers through the gaps to look at Connell.

"I see you spying on me. Just you keep your hands off my drink, I tell you."

"No chance," Sean laughs. "You having fun down there?" He sniggers at Connell as he continues to peer through the vent.

"Aye, so I am. Come on chuck us down a bottle. I need it for my nerves."

"Sean," I whisper as I indicate for him to step out of the room, which he does amongst screams of abuse. "This might be a good idea, if we can get him drunk then we can get him close to the thing."

"But the creature won't go in him if he's drunk. Anyway, we don't have an escape plan yet."

"I do *now* but you're going to have to trust me on this." I run back into the cellar. "Connell, we're taking a crate upstairs. I'll bring you some down afterward, okay?"

"Aye you will," he said. "Never had you down as a thief, Destiel."

"I will bring you some, you have my word. I won't let you down but yes, I have become a thief I'm afraid. Under the same circumstances you would…" Sean pulls me away mid-sentence and I call to Connell as we leave the room. "I'll be back," I tell him.

"Aye, big man, like I believe that," he says as I make my way out with a crate of his whiskey.

"What's the plan, Dest," Sean asks as soon as we are out.

"Come on, quick, I need you," I say as I rush upstairs. I hear him dashing up behind me.

"What *is* your plan," he says flinging the door closed behind us.

"The butterflies, Sean. There are arrow holes in the cellar walls where they get inside. It's easy for them to come and go from the garden from there and I guess they use it to nest, who knows. I didn't know there were air vent holes in the cellar through to the dungeon. This is how Connell knew we were there. The sound travels right through, perhaps he heard our whispers or maybe the light shone in on him. Either way, it doesn't matter. The point is, the butterflies can pass freely through these vents."

"I'm with you…" he replies as his eyes dart from side to side while he gets one step closer to my plan of action. He stares at me and I know he has guessed my idea, "We get the thing into a butterfly by scaring it into trying to escape right?"

"Yes, exactly. It will not attempt to separate from you and run of its own accord. It will need to be intoxicated and confused into believing it needs to tendril. This is what the machine part of it will do. It is programmed to tendril when under threat. This is what it does and it has no means to alter the encoding itself."

130

"So, we scare it and it tendrils out into the butterfly. What if it heads out one of the arrow holes and then escapes?"

"It won't. Not if we cover the holes from the outside." He nods in agreement and then I am jolted from my strategy as I remember my previous efforts to free the subject. I sigh wearily, "But then there is *something* against us."

"What is it? This has to work, Dest."

"It burnt up within a few minutes when it vined out into the mouse. The animal was so small that it just couldn't take the might of the Sior-Mabuz inside it"

"It doesn't mean it won't work. How long for a butterfly?" he asks. I have no real idea and, from here on, it seems to be guesswork taking the reins

"Thirty seconds, maximum," I say sadly, giving him my best estimate. "I'm sorry, Sean, I thought I had a plan. I hadn't thought it through properly. I've let you down again."

"Wait a minute. There's thousands of those things. What if it makes stepping stones of them while it makes for the slats to get out," he says enthusiastically, at which point, I pick him up and kiss him.

"You're a genius," I say, practically jumping for joy. "It could work, Sean."

"Like you said yourself, it didn't choose me just because I'm a pretty face." He rubs his fist on his collar as he compliments himself on his idea.

"You are so much more than that," I say as we smile at each other. "I'm going make sure you get out of there, Sean. We can leave this place forever, we can go anywhere we like after this. I love you so much."

"I love you too, Destiel," he says as he flings his arms around me.

"Hey, we're not there yet, Sean. Come on, we need to get the rest of this sorted out. There isn't much time left."

"You worry too much."

"So, what happens when the butterfly escapes?" I ask as I ponder the situation. "I think, it will either attempt to get inside an animal outside, or morph back into itself when it can't find a host."

"Oh no, no, no," Sean grins. "Destiel, you're missing the point. The butterfly finds a big, fat, ugly, Scottish Laird lying drunk in a whiskey cellar."

"Sean," I grin, "You're amazing." I kiss him again. "Today yes, sunrise today, come on Sean?"

"I think I can manage that," he says as he looks at the clock. We have around five hours of darkness left. "There's just one problem. How are we going to scare the crap out of the Sior-Mabuz?"

"We'll think of something," I say as I make for the door.

"Where you going?" he asks.

"To fetch a wee dram, for the big man," I say with my best Scottish accent.

"I'll come with you. We're going to have to get him moved to that whiskey cellar and he might try something dodgy. Dest, be careful down there, we don't know what he will do."

When we arrive in the dungeon, we find Connell waiting impatiently for us. He has beads of sweat forming on his ruddy complexion, and he appears to be quite agitated. He wants his drink and he wants it now. The desire to satisfy his craving has consumed this man's whole mind. What a terrible affliction he has to endure. It must be a dreadful burden to be so reliant on such a devastating substance. I remember his liking for fried food also, and I am convinced this man has no control over his lifestyle choices, or if he has then he has made very foolish decisions.

"Took your time didn't you," he asks as he runs his filthy finger around the inside of his sweaty collar. "Hey, where is it?" he grunts upon noticing our hands are empty.

"Connell, we have a plan," I say.

"Give me my whiskey," he croaks, "and turn that light off in my cellar. What are trying to do, get me killed?"

"All in good time," I reassure him. "Connell…"

"Please, Destiel, please, I beg you. I'll do anything, just don't leave that light on, please," he screeches.

"Connell, listen…" I continue as I try to tell him he has to move up into the cellar.

"Hold on a minute, Dest," Sean says as he holds up his hand. "Connell, why are you so bothered about the light?"

"You know why, you asshole."

Sean looks at me, "You talk to him."

"You mean the butterflies?" I say thinking of what Sean had said about them flapping around his head. "But surely they are *attracted* to the light. They would leave this dungeon for the light in the cellar. It would help you if we left it on."

"Don't give me that crap. I know what you're trying to do. You know exactly what I mean. You know that thing freaks out in the light." He points to Sean and grimaces. We don't know what he is talking about. Sean and I look at each other with puzzled expressions. "Aye that's right, I know what you're up to."

"I don't and this is getting irritating. Just say it, Connell. What are you on about?"

"It's going to shit itself and go nuts."

"You're going to have to spell it out for me, Connell. I honestly have no idea what you mean."

"Look, it goes crazy whenever I come to my cellar for my stuff. It freaks out when the light goes on. I'm scared it'll escape, please," he begs. "Don't do it. You can stay here." Sean and I look at each other, both sensing a weakness in the Sior-Mabuz. We say nothing. There is no way we are about to tip Connell off to what we're doing.

"Well you won't have to worry about that," I tell him. "It won't affect you."

"You going to put me out of my misery then?" Connell asks, his eyes darting between Sean and me.

"We thought you'd like a new room," Sean says. "We got just the place, plenty to keep you company."

"What you saying?" He is becoming more distressed, which is making him so much more pliable. He's putty in our hands.

"We have a deal for you?" I suggest and suddenly, I have his full attention.

"Okay, I'm listening," he replies, seeming somewhat relieved he isn't about to be killed.

"You give us one more day and tomorrow evening we'll be gone. Don't worry, you won't have to stay in here tonight. We'll lock you in the whiskey cellar instead and you won't have to be in the same room as the Sior-Mabuz. Not only that but you'll get all the whiskey you can drink."

"And you'll let me out when you go? And I'll get both of you gone off my land?"

"Yes, you have my word," I reply. "I know of another location we will move to and you'll have your grounds back."

"Sounds good to me, let me out of this then," he says holding up his chained arms.

"Any funny business and you'll be back in here and we won't chain it down," Sean says and Connell nods acceptingly.

"I want some cushions bringing down as well, I want some sleep, I'm knackered. Oh and you can bring me some food."

"You want a tea cozy for your whiskey glass as well?" Sean asks as he rolls his eyes.

"Hey, I'm doing you a favour. All I want is something to eat. It's not much to ask is it?"

"Well if it'll shut you up," Sean replies. We agree to the requests and, surprisingly, Connell is very reasonable and moves to the cellar relatively moan free. It makes me feel almost bad for the guy. Once he is safely ensconced inside, we close the door and bolt it.

We make our way outside to the tool shed. One of our torches has stopped working and so I cling to Sean to ensure neither of us stumbles. The last thing we need is one of us injured and unable to walk. I enjoy the walk, in spite of everything going on around us. It's good to feel an icy breeze drift by. I am sheltered from most of it by Sean's warm body. The wind brings the scent of him to me and I am comforted. I always feel so secure and safe when he is with me. Soon, I will have this feeling always. We reach the shed disappointingly quickly and as I put the light on, I am hit by a revelation.

"I feel so stupid, of course it's afraid of light," I say. "How could I not have realized before now." I slap my head in frustration at my own stupidity.

"I don't get it, Dest, if it's afraid of light why does it hunt in the daytime?"

"That's natural light. It is the machine element of it which is afraid of light - artificial light. It goes crazy when Connell goes into his cellar because the beams streak through. It sees them and goes ape. It's instinct and it wants to escape. It wants to escape *anyway* but when the artificial rays give off the wrong type of energy, it just goes stir crazy. It's the leftover robot residue, the robot part of the creature believes its tendrils will be destroyed. Our own robot's emissions are very similar, and they also use these light rays to overcome opposing machines in the future. This creature has been pre-programmed and set to evade this energy at all costs. This is why it sleeps during the night, for fear of this light snaking its way into its mechanism if it were to encounter it. In short, it hibernates to keep safe, which is a component of many of these archaic robots."

"How come you didn't know this before now then?"

"Sean, that thing is permanently angry. Would *you* be able to tell whether it was screaming in rage or fear? It just didn't register, but it's so obvious now."

"Well, I hope you're right," Sean says as we search for useful items. We hunt quickly for materials, and find much of what we need. Combined with the stuff I found earlier I think we are set. Anything else and we will just need to improvise.

We dump the equipment and set to work immediately, we have relatively little time left. Sean heads outside and begins sealing the gaps in the wall, in the hope the Sior-Mabuz does not escape when in butterfly form. Not that it would have long enough before it burnt up, but we need to be sure. I open the cellar door and fling a pillow and packet of potato chips in to Connell. I then start barricading the door, fearing that the bolt may not hold the creature. I continue my work, in spite of yells from Connell asking what's going on. I try to tell him we are trying to make him secure but he has doubts and is under the impression we intend to leave him to die. He's sort of correct and I feel terrible, but this is something we need to do. He is the only person who has done anything to warrant this fate. It doesn't matter what he says now. As long as the switch takes place then we have nothing to fear. Once done, I sit on the floor and rest. I hope Sean makes it through this alive. I have dreamt of the moment of his escape for so long and I have already begun to make plans for our future life together. Losing him now would destroy me.

When Sean returns, we go down into the dungeon, where we quietly cover all vents but one. We need at least one gap for a butterfly to find its way to Connell. There is quite a tunnel through the vent but it does lead to the cellar. I hope the creature makes it through. I do not know what will happen if the Sior-Mabuz sheds a butterfly in this tunnel. I cannot bear to imagine. We leave the stepladder in place next at the last gap and sit the board down ready to be placed over the vent as soon as the butterfly enters the tube and, hopefully, finds Connell.

I rig a light in the exact position needed. It will shine directly onto the Sior-Mabuz. It is ready to be switched on when Sean is locked down. This should be enough to frighten the creature into action. I leave the jar of pupae I have collected near the harness, ready to be tipped out. I expect the creature to see it and spread its tendrils into one of them. Its energy will be enough to rouse the sleeping butterfly baby and provide the flight needed to find another insect. According to Sean, he is surrounded by them every night when he awakes, which means there are plenty around. We can only hope the thing is able to make it into one and buzz its way through the tunnel and into Connell. All is set and ready for our plan of action.

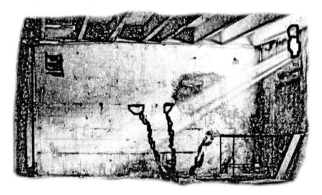

When we get back upstairs, having fully prepared, Sean begins to drink his whiskey. We have two hours in which he must get drunk enough to stun the Sior-Mabuz. It will instantly want to leave his body and, when it sees the light, it will want to flee as far from that place as it can.

"What if he doesn't find the chrysalis? What if he can't make it to the next butterfly?" Sean says. I can tell he is beginning to panic. I'm scared too, I'm used to dangerous situations but I've never had to save someone I loved before. I've never *loved* anyone before.

"Sean, I will use my telepathy to guide the insects. I have been trained to do this, although it has usually involved a willing participant and much effort on my part. I will help all I can as I try to guide the insect part of the newly evolved Sior-Mabuz/butterfly union. I do not know if I can do it but I will put as much effort into this as I can. I will sense when it has entered the vent and gone into Connell. As soon as this happens I will get into that dungeon and seal the gap. I will help you out straight after and lock the door. We will then race up the stairs and close the trap off. It can't fail if we stick to the plan."

"I'll keep that in mind." He smiles, "I hope it works, I think it means a lot to you."

"Of course it does, Sean. I can't be without you now."

"There's so much that can go wrong though," he says looking weary. I struggle to know what to say as I sit next to him. "Don't worry, we'll do it." It's all I can think of to comfort him. I take his hand. "I'll get you out. I'll protect you. I'll never let you down, Sean."

"I'm scared, Dest," he says taking hold of me and squeezing me tight.

"Me too." I know this next hour is the last time that I may ever see him alive again. I'm not going to tell him

140

that and, besides, I meant it when I said I wasn't going to let him down.

"If I don't come out of this, I want you to get the hell out of here. Don't let it take you. If you know that thing hasn't moved out of that dungeon, don't you come in there. You promise me, Destiel."

"You will come out."

"Promise me you won't come in there."

"I promise," I say before getting up and walking towards the window. I don't want him to see the tears building in my eyes. The truth is, I don't know if I can get him out, but I do know I will keep up my end and get those butterflies to that vent. I reckon we have a fifty/fifty chance at best.

It's not too long before the alcohol begins to have an effect. It's lucky Connell enjoys a whiskey and not wine. It's strong stuff and Sean is becoming a little drunk. I believe it is for the best as he will need something to help him relax. He is already on a small dose of painkillers and I imagine they are reacting with the alcohol too. It won't hurt and may even help. It's not as if he has taken enough to be detrimental to his ability to function. I get him two more to see him through the painful day ahead.

"Here, get these into you," I say. We only have a half an hour left." He takes a couple and I hope it will also speed along the intoxication. It isn't long before he is quite drunk. I like drunk Sean. If the mood is right, he can be kinda sweet when he's had a couple of drinks.

He lets the guard down and you get a glimpse of the man inside.

"Come here, Dest. You know I love you don't you," he slurs as he pulls me down onto the couch next to him. His breath stinks of whiskey but I kiss him anyway. "Don't ever leave me, you promise?"

"I won't, Sean," I tell him as we lean back and lie together. "I remember the first time I ever saw you, Sean. You were fighting that machine. I'd never seen a human do that before. Not with such primitive weapons."

"That's right, I remember. You turn up thinking I need help but I'd already killed it by then and I blow the tip of my gun like some sort of cowboy," he laughs. "You should've punched me then for being a smug asshole."

I laugh, "You were a bit of a show off back then but you were good Sean. I've never known anyone like you before. You're the bravest person I know," I say as I kiss the top of his head.

"I'll get like that again if you keep on like this." He takes another swig from his cup. "You know what, Dest, all this… it's been worth it. I'll let you into a little secret," he giggles drunkenly. "It's always been you, ever since that first day. I remember you just staring at me and everything around me went hazy. Everything but you and your blue eyes and your black hair. You were all I could see. I loved you then, and I love you now, and I always will. I promise you that." His eyes fill with tears and I am speechless. I begin to sob as we hold each other tightly. I kiss his lips and slide my hand up inside the back of his shirt to feel his warm skin. This is the greatest moment of my entire life and if it all goes wrong, I will remember his words forever. We hold each other tightly and share our final kisses before the clock forces us to break apart for what will ultimately be the most chilling fight of our lives.

Chapter 11

I help Sean to the ground floor. He is stumbling and slurring heavily but I manage to get him down the first set of steps to the halfway mark. When we arrive there, we are greeted by roars from Connell. Sean seems oblivious, which I am grateful for. I drown out his screams as we negotiate our way down into the dungeon. Sean is unable to help with the set up and so I must work quickly to ensure all is in place. I attempt to catch him as he flops onto the floor but I miss and he lands hard. I prop him up, make him more comfortable and secure him to the restraints. Once he is fastened safely, I check the light is in place ready for the Sior-Mabuz to be greeted by its rays upon waking. Sean is very drowsy but when I talk to him, he is mostly still coherent enough to be understood. I tell him that all is in place and we are ready.

"Get out, Dest," he slurs. "I can feel it coming."

"I'm going, Sean, I have set the butterfly pods here." I point to a scattering across the floor. There is a trail of them towards the vent. He briefly acknowledges this before closing his eyes. I put my arm around him.

"I love you, Sean," I say before kissing his head and walking towards the exit. I look back to see him open his eyes and I wink nervously.

"Goodbye, Destiel," he says.

"See you soon," I reply.

I push the bottom door closed, lock it and dash up the steps to the cellar door and lean against it. I hear Connell moaning but my ears won't seem to let anything in. The sound of my heartbeat is drowning most of the other noises out. I find myself sliding down the doorframe as I am overcome by exhaustion. I bury my head in my hands as I start to cry. I know I have to pull myself together if I am to see what's happening and direct the butterflies away from Sean and into the vent.

I take a deep breath and cover my ears, forcing my mind to go black. I say a thirty second mantra in order to reach the quieter, non-emotional part of my mind and, as I chant, I see the image of Sean contorting into the Sior-Mabuz. It is a sickening sight but I have found such a state of mind that I am disconnected enough not to be affected. It is as though I am watching a TV show. This is the deepest level I have ever reached and, as waves of indifference sweep over me, I am able to logically determine the thoughts of the creature. My mind has merged imagination with reason and I have become a medium between the creature and the butterfly chrysalis beside it.

I sense the creature's anxiety as its black hole eyes find the light. I am unaffected by its fear and remain calm whilst I mentally suggest it should attempt to escape by means of transference. I witness its aimless panic take shape and, in its delusion, it takes on my commands like they are coming from its own mind. It has gained my perspective and I own its thoughts. It starts to look around its surroundings, I know it is searching for the means to discharge itself. I keep all thoughts of Sean far from my mind and, because of this, the creature seems to be completely unaware of Sean's presence as it hunts for deliverance and discharge. I envision the chrysalis and I feel it's energy pull in the direction of the cocoon. He contemplates his next move and I push everything I have at the animal to give it the push he needs and then, I watch as it slides from Sean's body and into the pupae. Instantly the chrysalis bursts open and a hideously deformed butterfly emerges. I am momentarily distracted as I watch Sean's body fall to the floor.

I believe he is dead and then, I am snapped back into my mission as the creature looks back at Sean through its new, mesh-like, insect eyes. I perceive the butterfly ignite and start to burn as it is consumed by the Sior-Mabuz. I hear a faint squeal as the creature dives into another butterfly which glides by. That's two steps away from Sean, I think as, once again, I push from my mind the image of his lifeless body in the corner. I urge the Sior-Mabuz to find the vent and then, to my astonishment, I am pushed out of the equation as it takes on its own scheme to get out. I see the next flame-filled butterfly turn to cinders and drop like a puff of smoke, just as another one flares into life. I then watch as the butterfly trail blazes around the dungeon like rainbow firecrackers. I can do nothing but hope the sparkling path leads to the vent and the Sior-Mabuz finds its way to its new home.

I hold my breath, shaking as I root for the Sior-Mabuz to make its escape. Then, seemingly without reason, I lose contact. I am suddenly alone on the steps in the darkened corridor as I am pulled away from my vision. I wonder what has happened and then I hear Connell cry out.

"Get away from me," he screeches as a loud bang emanates from his cellar. I wait and listen to the commotion, hoping for signs that the transfer has happened. Soon, all goes quiet and I attempt to find a picture in my mind but none comes. I am worn out, I cannot find intuition. My sixth sense has left me, itself also burned up in the energy which bathes this burrow of despair. I stand up, wait and hope. I put my ear to the cellar door, just in time to hear the Sior-Mabuz let out a deafening scream. My head is jolted away from the door as it thrusts itself towards it in an effort to escape its new prison.

I stand dazed for a second, and my thoughts switch to autopilot as my mind yells at me to *get Sean*. I run towards the steps, tripping as I go and tumbling down the lot of them. I whack my head at the bottom and knock myself senseless but something keeps me going. I am running on pure adrenaline as I manage to stagger to my feet and climb the step ladder. I briefly look towards Sean and begin to breathlessly sob as I realize he is dead. I secure the vent, to ensure the Sior-Mabuz does not find another butterfly and arrive back inside the dungeon to take hold of me. I dismount the steps, wondering if it might be better that I die too. It even crosses my mind that I should uncover the vent again and allow the Sior-Mabuz its revenge on me. I cannot live without *him*, my Sean.

There is no point going on. I scream out in anguish as I approach my beloved Sean and feel for a pulse. I find none and, without his love to spur me on, I collapse in a heap beside him.

"Don't leave me, Sean," I beg as I hear the Sior-Mabuz growling. I remember my promise to him not to let it win and I stand up and yell at it to, "shut the hell up." I then lean over Sean and begin to bang hard on his chest. I fill his lungs with air but still he does not wake up. I grab him by the scruff of the neck and order him to wake up but still he doesn't respond. I loosen his clothing and remove his shoes to cool him before shaking him frantically. I even beg the God to help but, of course, he does not come to me.

I stand up and scream out again as I become dizzy and start to stagger around. I feel that my head is caught up in the energy of the butterfly death path, and then all fades away as I am whisked miles away in my time machine. I look around and am enveloped in the white light that is the essence of time and space. It's as if I have merged into it and have become time itself. I swirl high in the ether as I float through the light and am lowered to where Sean's body lies still. I see nothing but sense I am being taken down towards him. I know his face is before me and instinctively, I open his mouth and exhale the white light from my mouth into his.

As soon as the transfer has happened, I am instantly transported back to the dungeon as I fall into a heap beside Sean. I cannot hold on as I drift aimlessly in the memory of shifting times. I resign myself to Sean's death and allow my mind to hover, lost in the void surrounding me and then I hear him cough. It passes me by at first, and then, there it is again. I wrench myself from the vortex and manage to gain lucidity as my eyes clear. I am facing the door of the dungeon which disorientates me at first, and then I feel his hand on my shoulder.

"Destiel," he says weakly. "Dest, help me." I turn to see him attempting to stand as he is pulled down by the chains. I conjure all my strength and, unsure of whether it is all just an illusion, I fumble to free him. Everything is a blur as I lift him from the floor and stumble from the pit...

I place him gently down before turning to the door and slamming it shut and bolting it. I then lift him again and raise my heavy feet from one step to the next, passing the thuds of the thunderous Sior-Mabuz along the way. After what seems an eternity, I arrive at the top of the steps. I lay Sean on the ground and then, with the last thrust I can muster, close the trapdoor and lock it firm.

He is out, Sean is out... and... he is breathing...

Chapter 12

I get him upstairs, take the rest of his clothes off and slip him into bed. He is fading in and out of consciousness. I make him as comfortable as I can before dashing to the kitchen to fetch him a drink. While I am there, I run a cloth under the cold tap for a few moments and then wring it out hard. He is semi-awake when I return to his bedside. I gently dab his brow with the cloth as I try to cool him down. He is very feverish, I imagine the shock has caused his system to go into overdrive as it tries to keep him alive. I guess the body has been attacking the Sior-Mabuz like a virus. It is trying to obliterate the worse infection of his entire life and, up until now, has been fighting a losing battle. Well, not anymore, if there's one person who can make it through this, Sean can.

"I dreamt God saved me, Dest," he croaks. "I was in total darkness and couldn't get out… he brought me back." He grabs my arm weakly as he tries to get my attention. I turn to him as his eyes roll in his head. He blinks a few times and then manages to focus on my face. "He looked just like you and he saved me from the darkness… he…"

"Don't talk now. Here, drink this," I say offering him the water I have brought. He pushes himself up with my help, takes a sip and then lies down again.

"It hurts so much, Dest," he says as he thrashes about, struggling to find comfort. I fetch him some painkillers and he manages to take them with a large gulp. He starts sweating profusely and his face turns deathly pale. I think he is going to bring the pills back up, but instead he lies back and closes his eyes. I fetch some more water, and this time add some sugar to it so he has some energy to beat this. It seems to calm him and I wonder if he has been suffering from hypoglycaemia and this is why he has been eating so much. I watch him for a half an hour, the colour is coming back to his face a little and his breathing pattern is returning to normal. I wait for a little longer before deciding he is going to make it. He is going to be okay. He just needs to sleep and let the pain subside.

I am uneasy but I leave him for a few moments while I go into the bathroom and lock the door. I feel weary and, as I kneel on the tiled floor and fall onto my side, I begin to sob. The feeling is almost indescribable but I am torn between enervation and exhilaration. I am unable to move as I let my emotions flood out from the depths of my soul. I cry until I can cry no more. I don't know what happened and how I was able to revive Sean. I consider what happened and come to the conclusion that I have absorbed sparks of power from the momentum of time over the years. I have picked up specks from the abyss and now I have passed them onto Sean and regenerated his spirit back to life. It's all I can come up with to justify why he was dead and now he's not. Perhaps the energy transfer will have a lasting impact, I just don't know. This is something I have never encountered before. I am just eternally grateful he came back from wherever he was. I experienced his death once and it's not something I can ever go through again. I will keep him safe always.

I look in the mirror, I am covered in his blood and my tears. My eyes are so bloodshot from fatigue that they look almost violet. I shower, I don't want him to see the state I am in, or even know that I have been crying. I want him to be secure in my strength to protect him. I cannot let him down and no matter how I feel inside I will not let it show. I will be there for him whatever it takes. I go as fast as I can, I do not want to leave him for long. I put on clean clothes and do the best I can to pull on a brave face as I step into the bedroom.

"How are you?" I ask upon noticing that he is awake. I am surprised he is able to talk and is so alert. It must have shaken the ground he walks on to have survived such an ordeal, but this is Sean and he is far from just an ordinary person. I guess this is one of the reasons that the Sior-Mabuz sought him out.

"Destiel, what happened? I feel terrible," he says and then, to my surprise, he sits up. He appears to be getting better by the second. Even his wounds are healing with lightening speed. Perhaps the electrical transfer has speeded up his recovery processes.

"We did it, Sean," I smile as I playfully tap my fist onto his chin. "You and me together, we did it. We got that thing out of you."

"What thing?" he asks as he rubs his eyes. He seems confused, I guess it will take a while to sink in. It comes to mind that his memory has been wiped clean but I will not allow this to be true. He will not be an empty vessel. This would be like losing him all over again, and I just can't take that.

"The Sior-Mabuz thing," I say. "Don't you remember? We put it into Connell."

"Oh, yes. That's right, I had that monster living inside me. Is it gone now?" he asks. He is still muddled up and no doubt suffering the after effects of the drink too. It doesn't matter, at least he remembers something. He knows who he is and who I am, and that's all that matters.

"Yes, Sean, it's gone. I closed the vent behind it. It cannot escape. You are free and you are safe."

"Butterflies!" he gasps. "It went in a butterfly. I felt it go."

"Yes, Sean, that's right it took on the butterflies just like we thought it would." I smile as I hold his hand. "You're tired. Get some sleep. It'll all come back to you once you've rested." I kiss his cheek as he closes his eyes, and then I leave him to dream.

I know we still have one thing left to do once night falls, and that is to move Connell to the dungeon. After that, we must leave immediately, never to return to Hielan De'il Stravaig Castle. I prepare for our departure. Once set, I return to Sean, check he is okay and then get into bed beside him in order to rest. I fall asleep almost as soon as I lay down my head.

I wake up to realize night has come in fast. I check the time. It is 2am. I am aware that Connell will have morphed back into himself by now. I dread going down into that dungeon and I am reluctant for Sean to ever see that place again. I decide I will go alone and attempt to get Connell into the harness. Hopefully he will not put up much of a fight. He will be weakened and disorientated. After everything I have gotten through these past few days, this shouldn't be a problem and, should he put up a fight, I will have no option but to knock him out cold. I will drag him there if I need to. I hope he is compliant as I have truly had all I can take.

I creep from the bedroom, so as not to disturb Sean. I am torn apart inside to have to be the one to imprison Connell. Regardless of what he's done, it's a fate nobody deserves. I stride through the dark halls, feeling my way as I unwillingly navigate my way to the dungeon. The torch is failing fast and so I have decided to retain its battery power for the mission. I hope the power holds out so I do not have to do this in total darkness. I lift the trapdoor, dreading what lies ahead.

All is silent when I arrive inside the foul lair. I knock on the cellar door expecting a mouthful of abuse. There is no response. I shout to Connell but receive no reply to my calls. I panic that the Sior-Mabuz has escaped somehow. Perhaps the butterfly it inhabited found a way out and Connell's screams were that of a frightened witness. My thoughts turn to Sean and I wonder if he is safe from the thing while he is alone upstairs. I hesitate no longer as I barge into the cellar to find Connell sitting and shaking. He is hideously deformed. It would seem his unhealthy lifestyle has left him too weak to put up any type of defence against the creature. It is burning him up, just like it did the butterflies. I fear he will not live more than a few months at best.

"What do you know?" I ask. "Do you have any idea what has happened to you?"

"I don't feel well, Destiel," he replies. "I felt weird, like I was going to pass out and then I must have fallen asleep. I guess I drank too much It's a curse." He points to the bottles and I see that much is gone. I know from his description of events and his haggard appearance that the hand over did take place, the Sior-Mabuz did indeed enter him. However, I don't believe he is aware of this crushing fact.

"Please," he urges, pointing in the direction of the bottles. I fetch his drink to him, I see no harm in allowing him a little liquid tranquillity. I have a certain amount of sympathy for his predicament but he is responsible for this whole sorry mess and he will suffer the consequences. If this has to happen at all, then this is how it should be. My judgement tells me to hide the truth from him. It would do him no favours to enlighten him to his fate. I sit and talk to him for a while as he drinks. I understand that this man is an alcoholic and so I simply wait until he is drunk and then

I drag his weakened frame downstairs. It's relatively easy and I had not envisioned it being so simple a task.

Once he is secure, I go back up to his whiskey cellar and lug crate after crate to the dungeon. I believe he will at least be grateful for small mercies. He will have enough alcohol to last him for some time to come. I say goodbye to him and I pledge that I will return with more alcohol in the future. It might not be much but I feel better that I am able to do something to ease his existence. I walk out of the door without looking back.

It's around 6 am when I arrive upstairs again. I peek in at Sean, who is still sleeping and then make myself a drink as I wait for him to wake up. I mull over what has happened, I've hardly had chance to breathe lately. The time spent at Hielan De'il Stravaig has been draining for everyone. I thought I would feel more at peace than I do. I thought I would be thrilled to be free from this place but I am not. This time with Sean has been the best and worst time of my life. Part of me wants to go and part of me wants to stay. The trauma is over and we can at last be together, but there is still a yearning to stay and be alone, just the two of us as it has been ever since we grew closer. I begin to wonder whether Sean and I could stay here forever. Keep an eye on Connell and enjoy the seclusion of the castle. During the times when we have been able put the whole nasty situation aside, we have been as close as two people ever could be. I don't want to let that go and, as strange as it might sound, I don't want to leave the castle.

I go to the bedroom and snuggle up next to Sean. I sense he is beginning to wake up and I want to be the first thing he sees when he opens his eyes. I wonder if he would consider staying on here. Somehow I doubt it. I lean over and kiss him to help him wake up. He stirs and then opens he eyes as he pushes me away. I think he is still a little confused and so I put my arm around him.

"Give me some space, will you?" he says, sounding a little more than irritated.

"What's wrong, Sean, are you okay?" I ask, worried sick that he is slipping into reverse gear and falling further into mental and physical decay.

"I will be if you'll leave me alone," he snaps. "What are you doing in here anyway? If we've gotta share this bed at least move over there."

"Are you angry with me?" I ask. I'm concerned that I have done something wrong but I can't imagine what. He sits up, now wide awake.

"What you doing grabbing me like that, Destiel?" he says curtly. He looks really pissed at me.

"Why are you being like this, Sean? I've been through hell for you." I just don't understand what's happening here. Why is he being so hostile towards me? It's like he's had a personality transplant or something. I give him the benefit of the doubt. I guess I wouldn't be full of the joys after going through what he has.

"Yeah and I'm grateful for everything you've done for me, Destiel. I just want to be left alone. I don't want you in bed with me, if that's okay!"

"I get it, Sean, but yesterday you told me you never wanted us to be apart again," I move forward and try to kiss him. He pushes me off.

"What do you think you're doing?" he asks as he throws me a look I've never seen from him before. It's almost as if he hates me.

"I love you, Sean, please?" I place my hand on his arm and try to pull him to me but he blocks me from getting close.

"What? You love me do you?" he replies as he laughs. It's like he's mocking me. "Well, I ain't that way pal."

"Sean, do you remember us being together?" I say, recalling his memory lapse from earlier. I hope this is the concussion talking and once he regains clarity, he will remember everything.

"No, are you kidding or what?"

"I'm not. We love each other. You told me you did, Sean."

"You must have dreamt it," he says getting out of bed and picking up his clothes. "I'm going for a shower. Don't touch me again."

I move towards him. He puts his hand up to stop me and then leaves the room.

"Sean," I all after him.

"I mean it, Destiel," he shouts back at me. I don't know what to do. I sit on the bed with my head in my hands. I am devastated.

I can't believe Sean has forgotten everything we've said to each other. How could he do this to me, he's ripped me apart. I wonder if he ever meant a word of it when he cared so little that he just forgot all about us. It's like it just fell out of his head. Even if he has no memory, how could he be so callous towards me? I'm so hurt I can hardly stand it. He'd remembered some of the horror that had taken place but has completely blanked our relationship from memory. I debate with myself as to whether it may return sometime soon but I am not hopeful. I stand up and head to the kitchen to find something for breakfast, perhaps he is famished and after a good feed and some coffee he will start to feel normal again. I try to assure myself that he is simply concussed and that the missing parts will soon slip back into place.

I manage to create something suitable that will do until I can get more food for us. I call to him and he appears in the doorway looking fresh and clean. I want so much to hug him but I dare not.

"Thanks for this," he says as he sits down to eat. He doesn't even look at me.

"You're welcome," I reply as I also tuck into the little food I have taken for myself.

"Look, Destiel. I appreciate what you've done for me. I just can't do that stuff with you. I'm sorry if I've done something to make you think anything else. You're done in… are you sure you didn't imagine it? I mean, it was a hell of a thing going through that every day. It couldn't have been easy for you either."

"So you remember being inside the Sior-Mabuz then?"

"Well, I'm not likely to forget ripping out the throats of half of Glasgow am I?"

"That wasn't your fault." He is still feeling bad about what happened back then but he needn't. "Do you remember the nights?" I look at him to see if there is any spark of recognition and I try to read his mind but the barricade is as strong now as it ever was. He isn't woozy, he's completely sound in mind again. There's nothing hidden from him and I determine that the memory loss has occurred simply from his desire to forget all about what has happened between us. It seems I was right, I was a convenient stopgap. Something to cast all his anxiety on. Nothing more than a big cushion of love to get cosy in while he awaited his death.

"It's sketchy but yeah, I remember the creature leaving me and you helping me upstairs to sleep but not much else. Must've been boring for you stuck here alone whilst I slept. You should've got outta here. You were not sent back to nursemaid me."

"I couldn't leave you, I care for you too much." I watch him as he sighs hard and chucks his fork down.

"When did you get that way, Dest? I mean, come on, what is this?"

"Since I fell in love with you. You love me too. You told me."

"Yeah course, I did," he replies as he sits back and glares at me with a riled up, indifferent, look about him. He exhales loudly and rolls his eyes.

I can't believe he is saying this and I wish that he had never changed back. I never thought I would think this but I wish the Sior-Mabuz was still around. At least he was nice to me then. I was right, in his fear and confusion, he was clinging to me out of despair. So much so that he has blotted it out completely. I have lost him.

"It's okay, Sean. You're probably right. I guess I wanted it so much I dreamt it happened. We're both frayed. Can we still be friends?"

"Yeah course, just no more funny business though," he says getting up and slapping my back as he walks off.

When he returns he is wearing a hooded jacket. I suppose it belongs to Connell because it's way too big for him. It doesn't suit him. So much about him has changed in just a few hours. I can't help but feel a bitterness towards him in my heart. He sits down on the couch and puts his shoes on. I begin to panic that he is leaving, I can't just let him go like that. I quickly jump onto the couch next to him.

"Please don't leave," I plead. "Stay here with me, we can be together all the time now. Just the two of us. Don't walk away from me, Sean. I can't lose you."

"You don't have me. I gotta life. I'm not sticking around this medieval dump any longer than I have to. Let's just get him chained up and get the hell out of here. I want to go home."

"I've already done that. He's secure. He won't be going anywhere for some time that's for sure. I wanted to save you from the stress of seeing that place again. It nearly killed you, Sean."

"I appreciate that, man. I really do." He sighs as he runs his hand through his hair. He is thawing towards me, I can tell. "I'm grateful for everything and I mean that, Destiel, I really do."

"Where will you go?" I ask, knowing it is none of my business. He's made it crystal clear how he feels about me.

"Home of course."

"I mean from here?"

"I'll get there somehow. Look, I'll see you around, Bud, okay?" He picks up his bag and flings it over his shoulder and onto his back. "I wouldn't hang out here too long if I were you though. It's not a good place, and it could be you next time." He attempts to stand up and I grab him and press my lips to his.

He does nothing to resist my advances for the first few seconds of our kiss, and I think he has relented from his desire to leave, but then he pushes me aside.

"I told you not to touch me" he says as he sits forward and puts his head on his hand.

"I'm sorry," I tell him. I watch helplessly as I wait for him to walk away from me. I expect him to stand up and leave but then he turns to me and smiles.

"There's things I want, Dest," he says as he once again takes his eyes away from me. "I don't know what went on here, my memory of it all is vague. I know you think this would work but it wouldn't. I want a family of my own someday. I just want to be normal for once. I'm tired of all this. I'm sick of fighting and wandering about like some kind of drifter. It's gotta stop."

"Then don't fight this, stay with me. We don't have to stay here, we can go anywhere, Sean. Just name the place."

"I don't remember it, Dest, I'm sorry. I don't want it, any of it. I wouldn't like it to cost us our friendship but if there's a choice to make then I'll make it."

"I understand, Sean. I value your friendship above all else."

"I don't want to lose you, Dest. I need you around but I can't be what you want me to be."

"We should leave, Sean," I say, making the ordeal easier on him.

"We'll row across that lake and then go our own separate ways for a while, you cool with that?" he says and I nod. What else can I do? I wonder to myself where he will go from here and how he will get there. Perhaps he will steal a car and make for London.

"No, I'm not going to steal a car," he laughs. "I'm going to hitch a ride to Glasgow and get a flight."

"What?" I say turning swiftly towards him. I'm sure I never actually said that out loud.

"You asked where I was going and I said…"

"No, I didn't ask, Sean. I thought…"

"Huh?"

"It doesn't matter," I reply. He evidently has no idea what I'm talking about. I'm absolutely sure I never uttered a word but I'm beat. Perhaps I did say something. I decide to find out what's happened. I conjure a question in my mind – *Shall we check on Connell before we go?* I think it as strongly as I am able to.

"No, if you say he's secure, I'll take your word for it, Dest," he replies. He answered. He knows what I'm thinking. It seems Sean has developed some sort of telepathy. It must have been the energy transfer which caused this new phenomenon to manifest itself in him. It's there within everyone but can usually only be awoken under certain circumstances and, for most, it just simply never happens. I wonder if I am able to transmit feelings of love to him in an effort to win him back, but then decide this is a useless tactic. You can't force someone to love you and, besides, I want him to be with me because he wants to, not because I have remotely messed with his mind. I so wish he had never been freed from the grip of the Sior-Mabuz and I feel disgusted with myself for thinking such an awful thing.

Our relationship is gone forever, this I know. I have to learn how to be alone again. I had hope these past few days. Sean had renewed my zest for life, he had become everything to me but the time has come for me to say goodbye to the one person who made my life complete. I will never love again and, worse than that, I will never leave the confines of the year 2035.

The only thing left to do is say goodbye...

Epilogue

We leave straight away and take the boat. I savour the journey, as arduous as it is, because these are the last few moments we will spend together. Why doesn't he remember? Will the jigsaw piece itself together eventually? Will he ever come back to me? It is all I can hope for as I am now stuck in this time zone forever. I have turned my back on everything for him and now I am alone again. Our fates lie in opposite directions. It was not for us to be together but for me to be abandoned. I believe this is my punishment for having disobeyed the God. I must pay the price. I think I would rather go home and pay the penalty with my life because a destiny without Sean, is a destiny far more frightening.

We get to the other side and say our goodbyes. We stand and look at each other for a moment and I make a mental note of how he looks. Never more beautiful, his brown hair falling beneath his hood and framing his sparkling eyes. His skin is fresh and rejuvenated. He looks so young and there is no sign he has ever been through this whole terrible ordeal. He smiles and I smile back. My heart cannot take much more of this punishment and I hold out my arms to him.

"May I hug you before you leave," I ask and he throws his arms around me and pulls me closer than he ever has before. I feel the sorrow that floods his mind and I know he wishes he wasn't hurting me this way but he has no choice.

"Go carefully, Sean, you've been through so much. Take it easy now."

"You take care of yourself, you hear, and you know how to find me if you need me. I appreciate all you've done for me. You're a good friend, Dest. Hell, you're my best friend."

"You take care too, Sean," I say as he starts to walk away. I hesitate and then grab his arm. He turns to me and smiles. "Don't ever forget I love you, Sean."

"I won't, I promise," he replies as he lingers for a moment longer. I notice his eyes filling with tears and then he pulls away from me and I do the hardest thing I have ever done... I watch him walk out of my life.

He gets just a little way into the distance and I see a car stop. He leans in the window and a moment later opens the door. He glances back in my direction. I wave to him and he waves back.

"You coming or what, buddy?" a voice from the car calls. I see Sean grab a hold of the door, and then he hangs back. I flap my hand to indicate that he should hurry.

"Don't be a stranger, Destiel," he calls out to me as I see a tear roll down his face.

"I won't," I reply... and then I hear his thoughts...

"I love you," he says...

About The Author

Jordyn Burlot lives on the South Coast of
England with her family.
"Destiel" is her debut novel and she is
currently writing her second.
She also hopes to write for
film and theatre in the future.

Copyhouse Press

London

Lightning Source UK Ltd.
Milton Keynes UK
UKOW04f2355181215

265022UK00001B/2/P